❦ SPARKS SHALL ❦
RISE

VISIONS AND ILLUSIONS

LINDSAY McCAFFERTY

⊹ SPARKS SHALL ⊹
RISE

VISIONS AND ILLUSIONS

Content Warning

Content dealing with hallucinations and derealization.

Sparks Shall Rise: Visions and Illusions

This work of fiction is not a substitute for real advice from licensed physicians, therapists, or mental health professionals. Any portrayal of medical practices or therapy is fictitious and not to be interpreted as accurate.

The story, names, characters, and incidents portrayed in this production are from the author's imagination and are fictitious. No identification with actual persons (living or deceased), places, and events is intended or should be inferred.

First Edition (2022)

Cover, Map, Logo & Title Pages designed by MiblArt

Interior formatting made using Atticus.

ISBN-13 (Paperback): 979-8-9854011-0-3

authorlindsaymccafferty.com

PREFACE

I originally started writing this book after publishing the first edition of "Reawakened Flames." I stopped when I realized I needed to redo the first book. When I came back to this story, I had only written up to the climax—forty-five pages in.

Up until I was sure the story would break one hundred pages, I worried every day that I wouldn't be able to achieve it. The story was not flowing like the first one, and I struggled to come up with new content. I managed to reach my goal anyway and surpass it.

I also worried that I wouldn't be able to write the second book. What if I started the series and then couldn't follow through? I had never finished one before. I always thought I would write a fantasy trilogy, but this series is much longer than I ever imagined. There are so many storylines and characters still to write about. Disappointing myself and you, dear reader, are the last things I want to do.

That is what drives me to keep working hard on this series. I guess this is a lesson in never giving up, even when you are afraid that you will fail.

Keep pushing forward. You may end up surprising yourself.

Thank you to my editor, Kathy Bosman, for once again improving the book and teaching me more about writing. And thank you to MiblArt for creating another beautiful cover that surpassed my expectations, updating the map, and designing a title page.

Pronunciation Guide

Ehckrist – Eh-krist
Hanarthar – Haw-nar-thar
Landaro – Lan-dar-oh
Lythannen – Lih-than-nen
Torrannon – Tor-ran-non
Wierlling – Weir-ling

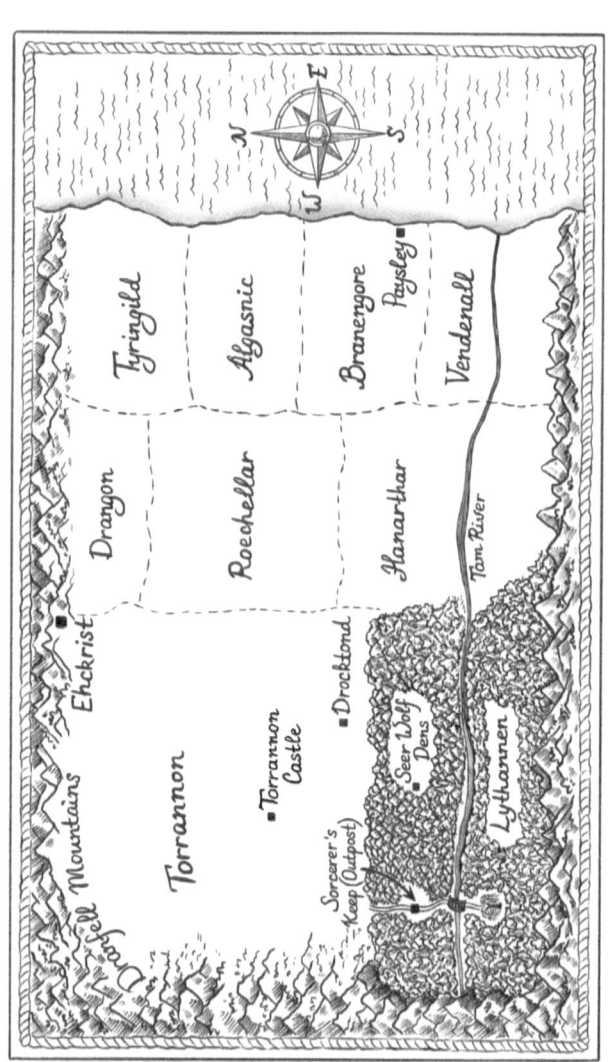

ONE

I N THE CLEARING, A breeze whistled through dying grass stalks and kicked up a cloud of dust. Dead, shriveled leaves and pine needles scraped against each other in the trees. A gust of wind made a shower of them fall to the forest floor. The trees were nearly bare. Even the pine cones were gone.

All the other foliage had withered away, leaving the forest hollow and lifeless. No creature stirred. The air was devoid of any scent besides decay. A shadow fell over the forest as angry storm clouds approached.

A seer wolf named Vision lay under an oak tree. She had white fur and blue eyes.

Vision shut her eyes and ran a paw across the ground. She repeated this several more times, pushing her paw down harder with each scrape. When she opened her eyes, reality blinked back into existence.

Puffy clouds sailed lazily across the sky. Vibrant green leaves and pine needles rustled in the wind like roaring waves. Branches creaked and scratched against each other. Cicadas buzzed. Birds sang their melodies and took off in flurries of feathers.

A squirrel scurried up a beech tree, and a hedgehog nosed through the grass next to a blueberry bush. Vision inhaled the numerous scents of the thriving summertime forest. It was hot, but she was cool enough in the shade where she could feel the wind.

A curious hummingbird fluttered over and hovered in front of her nose. She stayed still so as not to scare it. The little bird studied her for a few moments and then flew to a firebush. She didn't know why her parents had named her Vision when she couldn't always see reality in front of her.

Sometimes seer wolves had issues called mental illness, a word they had learned from the humans. That's what she had right now—she was sure of it. Hallucinations weren't something every wolf experienced.

Vision stood and shook off. She wavered with dizziness. It took her a moment to reorientate her mind and her body. The hallucination had been intense—the type that was harder to break out of and recover from. Luckily, those didn't happen often.

The intensity of the hallucinations varied. She might just see a packmate walking by when no one was there, or part of the forest would morph into a rocky landscape in front of her. A step into dew-covered grass created the illusion of a pond instead of a clearing. Other issues included hearing and smelling things that weren't there.

Running a paw across the ground—to feel the rough scrape of dirt, grass, or stones against her pads—shaking her head, or closing her eyes for a moment normally grounded her back to reality. A sound might also snap her mind out of it.

Earlier, another hallucination ruined her hunt. Vision had been tracking a rabbit. She'd poked her head around some rosemary shrubs and saw what she thought was the rabbit sitting next to a magnolia tree. She crouched and stalked closer and closer. Then she blinked, and her prey disappeared. Twigs cracked behind her, and the real rabbit burst out from the rosemary patch. She never caught it.

Vision yawned. She hadn't slept well last night. Her nap earlier hadn't made a huge difference either. She checked the clearing one more time to make sure it was real. The scene remained beautiful, as it should be. Vision shuddered. She never wanted to see the forest so barren and desolate.

Following a trail, where the seer wolves had trampled the ground down so much that they created a path, she headed back to the dens. She stopped when the trail split into three.

Normally, Vision could practically navigate the forest with her eyes closed. When she and her brother, Thorn, were pups, her parents took them all over the eastern part of Lythannen until they knew every tree and stone like the backs of their paws. Now, it wasn't so easy.

On one occasion, Vision had come to what she thought was a fork in a trail. She blindly went down one of the paths and walked straight into a tree. A sore nose and snout aside, she now sometimes questioned which trails were real and which might be hallucinations. She also had to pay attention to not follow ones created by other animals.

Vision took a breath and scratched each front paw across the ground. She gave herself a few moments to make sure she was thinking clearly. Nothing seemed out of the ordinary.

She stared at the trails and made sure she recognized them. One should lead toward the northern edge of Lythannen and Torrannon beyond it. Another trail should lead south toward the Tam River and the Dranfell Mountains. The last trail should lead east toward the dens as long as she didn't overshoot them and end up in Hanarthar. She especially didn't want to get turned around and go west toward the sorcerer's keep.

Vision scraped her front paws across the ground one more time and inhaled the forest scents. Satisfied that she was present in reality, she took the eastern trail.

TWO

WHEN VISION REACHED THE dens, relief washed over her. The ground rose and then sloped down into a circular dip in a clearing that had allowed the seer wolves to dig dens into the low slopes.

A long time ago, a den would just be used for a pregnant female and her pups. The rest of the pack slept outside. After the seer wolves gained their powers, they all felt safer sleeping in dens at night.

Vision sat on the top of the hill. The main den site was in front of her, and there were two similar dips on either side. Each site had fifteen dens, but most of the wolves slept in the main one. The pack wasn't at the number it used to be.

A large, smooth-topped rock jutted out from the hillside of the main den site across from Vision. The pack leader addressed everyone from there. A wolf with sandy-colored fur and brown eyes sat on it. She was Haven, the pack leader and Vision's mother. Her mother's brother, Pine, a light gray wolf with green eyes, stopped below the rock to talk to his sister.

A wolf brushed past Vision. He had gray fur and yellow eyes. He was Arrow, her father's brother.

The den sites hummed with activity. Everyone was home from their missions. Tonight, at the full-moon ceremony, they would receive new visions, and most of the pack would head out again.

Right now, the seer wolves ate, napped, sunned themselves, played, groomed, or chatted with each other. Pack life was simple. Besides the visions, the wolves hunted and looked after their own. They could live up to one hundred years.

Thorn padded across the clearing. He had brown-and-black fur and amber eyes. Thorn and Vision were from the same litter, but he was technically her older brother because he was born first. He would be the pack leader after their parents died. They had no other siblings.

Leadership passed from the pack leader to his or her mate, then through the pups, from oldest to youngest, and then to other family members. If all were dead or unfit to lead, and the pack leader didn't name a successor, then the pack chose a new one.

Squealing caught Vision's attention. A few pups wrestled in the middle of the clearing. Vision wanted so badly to have a litter of her own, but she was scared she might lose them by forgetting they existed.

The pups were real, right?

"Oh, no," Vision whispered.

Suddenly, the activity around the dens looked unrecognizable. Nothing in front of her had changed, but everything seemed as if it wasn't real.

It was as though she were only an observer and didn't exist within the world.

Vision scraped her paws across the ground, and she snapped back to reality. Another issue of hers. She called them disconnects because she felt as if she was disconnecting from reality.

Luckily, they didn't take as much effort to break out of. Vision sighed. She hated both of the issues. They made life so difficult.

Vision focused back on the activity around her. A dark brown wolf with green eyes poked his head out of a den and glanced in her direction. His name was Phase. He trotted toward her with his tail wagging.

He liked her—she knew that. Vision also had feelings for him, but he didn't know about the hallucinations and the disconnects. She was scared to tell him.

Phase climbed up the hill. "Would you like to go to the river with me?"

She nodded. "Sure."

Because she was tired, the mental illness was worse today. Vision had been having sleep problems ever since the hallucinations and the disconnects began a few years ago. It stressed her out, which made everything worse. Some time at the river with her friend would help her relax.

THREE

VISION FOLLOWED PHASE TO the nearby Tam River. She'd loved coming here ever since she was a pup.

Sparkling, clear water, that was particularly shallow, gently rushed and bubbled over smooth, gray stones. It was just as nice to lie on the grass and watch the water as it was to go in and cool off on a hot day or after a long hunt.

Vision padded across the stony bank. After lapping up some water to quench her thirst, she went out to the middle of the river and lay down. Cool water ran around her and through her fur. The sensation helped to ground her for the time being.

Phase lay across from her. "Are you ready for the full-moon ceremony?"

Vision shifted nervously. The hallucinations and the disconnect from earlier had put her on edge. The mental illness had steadily grown worse over the years, especially in the last few months. She didn't know how to gain control of it or make it stop. Neither of the issues had ruined a mission—yet. There had been a couple of close calls. Vision's deepest fear was that she might lose control of her mind entirely and no longer know what was reality.

"I'm just hoping for no warnings about any more possible wars," she said instead, which was true. The pack usually didn't all receive such a frightening sight.

Vision had probably been as nervous as her father while they waited to see if or when the rest of the pack would return from dealing with the invaders at the castle in Torrannon. She had stayed home, but her mother, Thorn, and Phase had all gone. Being in a battle would have been no place for her in her current state, anyway.

"The kingdoms seem to be at peace again," Phase said. "At least that's what I hear."

"Phase, do you ever wonder where our visions come from?" She was a curious wolf, always questioning things. Well, Vision used to be more curious. It didn't help that she was frequently exhausted from questioning reality.

Phase looked as though he was thinking it over. "Some kind of magic permeates this world, and I'm sure whatever created it is responsible for our abilities. Maybe we're left in the dark so evil people don't figure out how to harness our powers of foresight or, worse, how to access and control the source. Having that power could destroy the world as we know it."

Everything grew darker, and a chill passed through her that had nothing to do with the cool water. Vision looked up. A cloud blocked the sun. It moved away, and everything was bright again.

"Then let's hope that never happens," she said.

Phase's eyes became softer. "Enough about world-ending possibilities. Let's talk about something nicer, like us. We've been friends for a few years now. I think you know as well as I do that what we feel for each other has gone beyond just friendship. I love you, and I feel like it's time to ask this. Do you want to be my mate?"

Vision's skin tingled as excitement flowed through her, but thoughts about her mental illness made her mouth go dry. Her apprehension must have shown because Phase's face and ears fell. Vision didn't want to hurt her friend, but she had to think about what was best for her—for them.

She laid a paw on one of his. "I love you and care about you a lot too, but I don't feel ready to be your mate yet. I just need some time. This will be a big step for me."

Understanding dawned in Phase's eyes, even though he didn't know the real reason for her hesitance. He nodded. "Of course. Take all the time you need. I don't want to rush you into anything."

"Thank you." Vision stood and shook off. "Race you back to the dens?"

"You're on."

While they ran, Vision was aware of the grass and the dirt under her paws and the undergrowth raking through her fur. She let her guard down and felt normal for a few moments. The joy in Phase's eyes made her remember a time when her life wasn't as complicated. Vision wished she could return to it and once again be a normal seer wolf. She wanted to be as confident, excited, and happy as Phase.

The hallucinations and the disconnects constantly held her back. She hoped that one day she could feel free again so she could be with Phase and have the family she always dreamed of.

FOUR

THE FULL MOON GLEAMED. Vision glanced around at the forest and spotted movement. A shadowy figure that looked like a panther skulked around some bushes in plain sight. No one else seemed to see it. Vision blinked, and the panther was gone. It didn't appear again.

Panthers were able to disappear from sight in the shadows, but this one couldn't have been real. Someone else would have seen it or smelled it. The wind was blowing in their direction.

Panthers didn't enter the seer wolves' territory anyway. Her kind and their kind didn't care to interact. She'd only seen one once in the distance. The panther had just been an orange-brown streak that sprinted across the corner of a field, but she still recognized its outline. Their fur could be black, orange-brown, or blond.

Vision tried to keep her focus away from the shadows in the forest, which could trigger hallucinations. Nighttime made them worse. She stepped closer to Phase so she could feel his fur brush against hers.

The seer wolves gathered in a glade across the river from the dens. This used to be an old rendezvous site where pups grew up until they were old enough to travel and hunt with their pack. After the seer wolves gained their powers and all the packs merged into one, this glade became the place where they received visions.

The full moon used to mean nothing more than a brighter night every month. Now, the seer wolves had a more powerful connection to it and instinctively knew the correct night to receive visions. Everyone able to travel came. Wolves would rarely still be away on a mission during this time.

Vision remembered when she was over eight weeks old and able to accompany the others to the glade for the first time.

That full moon eight years ago, she'd trotted to keep up with her mother's longer stride. Vision and her brother had been carried across the river so they didn't get soaked and cold, despite their protests.

This was her first time walking through the forest at night, and although she wanted to run around and explore, she had to stay with the pack. Her father, Hunter, who had dark gray fur and golden eyes, stayed behind them to make sure Vision and Thorn didn't fall behind or try to wander off.

She had something on her mind. "Mother, why are visions and going on missions so important?"

Thorn pricked his ears up to listen in.

"Because we have a very special role in this world, my darling," her mother said. "A long time ago, the full moon shone larger and brighter than has ever been witnessed, and wolves were granted foresight. The phoenixes are the diplomats of the world, but we are the guardians. We take what we see at each full moon and do everything in our power to make sure it is used for good."

"Why were we chosen?"

"I don't know, but we were. This is our duty now, and we carry it out with honor."

Vision still wasn't satisfied. "But why is it our duty?"

Her mother had a thoughtful expression and didn't answer for a moment. "Because we have a connection to this world and its inhabitants that is far deeper than other creatures that don't have magic. By acting on the visions we receive, we have a meaning to our existence beyond just hunting and surviving. The phoenixes and...most of the humans respect us because of this."

The hesitance in her mother's voice when she mentioned the humans alarmed Vision. She had liked the few who she had met so far. Although the seer wolves preferred to keep to themselves in Lythannen, they had amicable relationships with the humans. Healers from nearby villages helped when wolves were injured or sick.

Thorn glanced at Vision with widened eyes and then looked at their mother. "Which humans don't respect us?"

Vision was unsure if she wanted to know the answer.

Her mother gave them a reassuring expression. "Don't worry, little ones. That was a long time ago. There's little danger from humans to us now."

They arrived at the glade, and Vision was mesmerized by the full-moon ceremony. Even though she wasn't old enough to fully participate, everything was new and exciting. She couldn't wait until she turned two years old and was able to receive visions.

Now, because of the mental illness, a simple and normal way of life had turned into a complicated mess and caused more anxiety than enthusiasm.

As she got older, Vision learned about the pack's darker past with humans. The seer wolves used to number more than five hundred strong but dropped to half because of years of being hunted by and having conflicts with greedy sorcerers wanting to harvest their magic.

The phoenixes had been in danger too, but their home was inaccessible. They could also stay relatively safe in the skies. The seer wolves weren't so lucky. During those dark times, even going on missions had been dangerous.

A great act of bravery and the killing of the sorcerer, who had lived in the old outpost in Lythannen, secured a safer future. Landaro, the leader of the phoenixes, forged a stronger alliance between his flock and the seer wolves. But the damage had been done to the pack's numbers. The wolves were still slowly recovering.

The humans believed the pack only had less than one hundred members left. The seer wolves kept their true number a secret so some sorcerers wouldn't be encouraged to take advantage of it.

Of course, Vision's mother wouldn't have wanted to scare her pups too much at that time by saying there would always be a danger from those people. Sometimes panthers also helped sorcerers, which could make them a threat to the seer wolves, too.

Vision sat next to Phase. Her mother took her place on a little hill at the front of the glade. A disconnect hit. Vision shifted closer to Phase again. His fur and the warmth from his body grounded her back to reality.

Phase glanced at her fondly and then lifted his head to the sky. Vision took a breath, ignored the darkness around her, and looked up at the moon.

Once the pack was settled, they all went silent. Seer wolves rarely all received the same vision like the one about Torrannon being invaded. Individuals or groups had different ones. What they saw might even be about themselves. It wasn't unusual for a wolf to not see anything, which was good because some always needed to stay behind to protect the dens.

Vision focused on the moon and waited. Sights passed before her eyes.

She saw a village by the ocean. A woman walked down a dock and boarded a ship. She wore dark purple travel clothes and a red hat. Her hair was put up in what humans called a bun. She also had a bag over her shoulder.

Then the sight changed. A man was crying and clutching a note. The vision ended. She lowered her head. Although hallucinations could cause dizziness, disorientation, and anxiety, what she saw was clear and sure.

From what she could tell, the mission was simple: locate a woman who was about to sail away, and inform her that someone was devastated she was leaving. If Vision was ever confused about what she needed to do, she could always ask for someone's advice.

Phase looked at her. "What did you see?"

"I have to stop someone from leaving on a ship," Vision said. "How about you?"

"I witnessed a farmer being robbed when he goes into a village. He fights the robber but is killed. He'll leave behind a family who needs him. I have to warn him to not take a shortcut through an alley. Then I'm going to alert the village guard and try to catch the robber. I'll need to leave in the morning."

As part of their powers, seer wolves had a special instinct that let them know when it was time to act on a vision and led them where they needed to go. Sometimes it was immediate, and sometimes it was delayed. Vision could also feel that she needed to leave soon.

She had been hoping Phase wouldn't have seen anything and been able to go with her. Some wolves, particularly siblings and mates, accompanied each other on missions if they could, and as long as too many weren't leaving. Thorn would probably have his own mission.

She would be alone on this one then. Vision tried to not look disappointed. She should be able to handle this on her own.

The rest of the wolves eventually lowered their gazes from the moon. Vision's mother was the first to let out a long howl. The others joined their voices with hers. This had become a tradition ever since they received their powers.

Vision needed to let her mother know that she was leaving. The pack leader kept track of who left and who returned. If one of the wolves took too long, a search party would be sent to find out what was going on. Her mother rarely left to fulfill a vision.

Phase and Vision walked side by side back to the dens. She forgot about the shadows as her mind whirled and her muscles tensed. Would she be able to keep control of her mental illness while on the mission, or would this be the time that something went wrong?

FIVE

AFTER A FIVE-DAY TREK to Branengore, Vision arrived at the bustling port village called Paysley. If she didn't have the magical instinct to guide her, the mental illness would surely have made her hopelessly lost while traveling.

Seagulls cried, and waves crashed in the distance. The salty air tickled her nose. A plethora of other scents filled her lungs, especially food. Spices, fruits, vegetables, bread, and the smell of fish flowed through the streets.

Her mouth watered, and she licked her lips when she picked up the aroma of cooking meat. She'd only stopped to hunt a couple of times on the way here, but she could only get a cooked meal if someone was willing to give one to her, which she'd never tried yet.

Vision wondered what kind of meat it was. The seer wolves never hunted the humans' livestock, so she didn't know how those animals tasted. One day, she would ask to try some meat. She didn't feel up to it today. Her hunts had been successful, so she wasn't starving.

Humans milled around, going about their business. Vision stuck to the edge of the road to stay out of the way. A banner flapping in the wind caught her attention. It had Branengore's standard, which was an animal called a gryphon on a red background.

It was a fierce-looking creature. The gryphon had the body of an animal called a lion and the head and front feet of an eagle. She wasn't sure if it was real or was just a myth. She never wanted to hallucinate a creature that looked like that.

The occasional passerby gave her a strange look. There were several kingdoms over the ocean and on the other side of the Dranfell Mountains. People from all over the world congregated in the port villages.

Humans who didn't know about seer wolves that well would probably find it odd to see one running around in a village. There might be other wolves in the world who didn't have the same magical powers.

Some people spoke in different languages. A few made hand signals to each other as though they were speaking. Her mother told her one time that deaf humans had developed a special way of communicating called sign language.

When wolves were deaf, they relied heavily on body language. The sign language seemed to be similar, although the humans had a greater range of words. Vision glanced at her front paws. Having hands probably helped.

The coastal villages and their sights, sounds, and smells might be interesting and fun to explore every once in a while, but she still preferred the peacefulness of the forest. Most of the wolves did their missions and then came straight back to Lythannen. They didn't usually linger too long among the humans. Vision broke out of her musings to focus on the mission.

She made her way through the crowds of people, still following the magical instinct and trying to not be stepped on. Later, she'd find a quiet place on the beach to relax for a while before she went back home. If only Phase could've come with her.

Vision made it to the docks, and the instinct faded. She didn't need it anymore. She just had to wait for the woman. Vision found a quiet corner across the street where she could keep watch.

She couldn't wait on the docks because she didn't know what the whole ship looked like—only part of it. Also, too many people were entering and exiting the ships. She would get in the way and attract unwanted attention or distractions. This spot would work fine. The overhang of a roof shaded her from the hot sun.

Vision kept her attention on the street and scanned the crowd. After a little while, she spotted something red. It looked like the hat she'd seen in her vision. The crowd parted, and she spotted the woman she was looking for.

Vision made her way across the busy street. She jumped when a horse snorted right next to her, and the rider cut her off. After backing up a step, she leaped forward to avoid getting her tail caught in the wheel of a wagon.

She darted to the other side of the road. The woman stood at the edge of the docks, so Vision shook off and gave herself a moment to calm down.

She checked to make sure that her tail was still attached. Satisfied, she walked over to the woman and opened her mouth to speak. Someone briefly walked in front of her.

After she made it through, she shut her mouth and froze. The woman had been there, but now she was gone. Vision looked around. She couldn't have disappeared that fast. Had this all been a hallucination? Another instinct told Vision she was too late.

She bolted down the dock. A horse reared in fright, and she almost knocked over two or three people. She got stuck trying to slip through a crowd exiting a ship. By the time Vision stuck her head out of the tangle of legs, her heart sank.

She spotted the woman on the ship, but it was sailing away. Anger, shame, and disappointment rolled through her like a violent storm. Her legs shook so badly that she almost collapsed.

Just as she'd feared, she'd failed a mission because of a hallucination. This was horrible. Missions didn't always work out because every variable couldn't be controlled—and sometimes seer wolves made mistakes—but this shouldn't have happened. The hallucination was a variable she should've controlled.

What if this was a life-or-death scenario? Ships sometimes got caught in storms and sank, potentially killing all the passengers. It would be her fault if something tragic happened to the woman.

Vision didn't stay any longer. There was nothing more she could do. She hurried back to Lythannen. What a poor excuse for a seer wolf. How was she supposed to continue doing missions when she had to worry about losing her focus on reality?

SIX

FEAR AND PANIC SURROUNDED Vision. The ship that she'd seen leaving the docks swayed from one side to the other in the churning ocean. The edges came dangerously close to tipping into the dark abyss. Rain poured, lightning zigzagged across the night sky, and thunder roared.

The woman with the red hat clung to a stair rail, sheer terror on her face. A large, powerful wave struck the ship and tipped it over. Vision entered the water.

She couldn't tell which way was up. Then she was caught in the gaze of the woman floating below her. The expression of terror changed to rage. She morphed into something that more resembled a wierlling, and the woman shot upward.

Vision tried to escape, but it felt as though she was being restrained. She whined and fought. The woman was about to grab her.

"Vision!"

Her eyes snapped open to see the walls of the den that she shared with her family. Outside, it was sunny and calm. Vision flinched and tensed up when she realized someone held her down.

"It's okay."

She relaxed when she heard her father's voice and looked up into his worried face. His eyes were wide, and his ears lay flat.

"Are you with me?" he asked.

"Yes," Vision said.

Her father got off her. "You were thrashing around and whimpering. I didn't know if you were dreaming or having a seizure."

Vision sat up, but a wave of dizziness hit her. She still felt as if she were on the tilting ship. She'd had terrible nightmares since the mental illness began, but this one was the worst. At least, Vision hoped it was just a dream and not that something bad happened to the ship.

She'd watched a storm on the coast a couple of years ago. The wind and the churning waves were terrifying. That was probably the memory her mind wandered to in the nightmare. She couldn't bear the thought of the other possibility.

Her father quickly came over and let her lean on him as she swayed. "Are you all right?"

"Yes, I'm okay." Vision regained her balance and sat still. "It was just a bad dream."

"Do you want to tell me about it?"

Vision hesitated. She'd gotten back late last night and had been able to go to sleep without anyone asking about her mission. If she spoke about the nightmare, she might have to mention how she'd failed. She especially didn't want to explain why.

"It's nothing," she said.

Her father didn't look convinced.

Vision stood, luckily without falling right back down. "I'm going for a walk."

Before her father could say anything else, she left. Vision slipped out quickly so no one else could question her. Had the others heard her having the nightmare?

It was later in the morning, and a lot of the wolves were back at the dens. A few of them glanced at her, but no one approached. Right now, the pack was the most active early in the morning and late in the evening to stay out of the heat in the middle of the day. They used to be more active after the sun went down, but their whole routine changed after the wierllings were unleashed.

From time to time, those evil creatures strayed into the eastern part of the forest. Except for the full-moon ceremonies when most of the pack was present, it was risky to roam the forest at night, even in the eastern part.

The wierllings only hunted humans with mental illness and didn't bother the seer wolves unless provoked. But sometimes they would attack someone they bumped into for easy prey. That included the wolves. Although the wierllings and the seer wolves tried to avoid each other, it was still a perilous coexistence.

Vision went out into the forest. She walked until she calmed down. She needed to just accept that she'd made a mistake and move on, but it was hard. It didn't fix the issue of hallucinations and disconnects distracting her while on missions.

How would she control them in the future to prevent another failure? Vision didn't know what to do or to think. She needed to make this work, but she was scared of messing up again.

Rushing water startled her. Vision calmed down when she realized it was just the Tam River—not the ocean. She followed the sound and had a drink. The edges of the river had receded.

There had been no rain for a few weeks. Other bodies of water would also be drying up. There was a spring close to the dens that never dried up, so the wolves didn't have to worry about running out.

Cracks were opening in the ground, and the undergrowth was wilting and dying. Even though it wasn't midday yet, the sun beat down on her. Vision went back into the shade of the trees.

Deep in thought, she wasn't paying attention to where she walked, and one of her front legs bumped into a fallen tree. The log was rotting and had a blanket of moss on top of it along with a few mushrooms.

"I remember you," Vision said.

This was the site of her first hallucination in another hot, dry summer when she was a little over a year and a half. She thought back to that time.

Vision ran through the forest. It was nighttime, and the moon shone brightly. Her brother called her name. She stopped and looked around. She couldn't see Thorn anywhere. He called again, and this time, it was louder.

The forest disappeared, and Vision opened her eyes. It was still somewhat dark. But where were the trees? Where was the moon? It looked like a wall of dirt and rocks in front of her. That couldn't be right.

Something jabbed her shoulder. "Hey, wake up."

Thorn sat next to her. He cocked his head to the side. "You were looking at the wall of the den as if you've never seen it in your life."

Vision shook her head, and her mind caught up with her. "I was still half in a dream."

She got up, stretched, and followed her brother outside. It was cloudy and windy. With any luck, it would rain. They had been in a drought for over two months.

The other wolves were beginning to wake up. The early morning scene should have felt familiar, but something wasn't right. She just couldn't pin it down. Vision shook off. She must not be awake and aware enough yet.

As she and her brother romped through the forest, something still bothered her. Something had changed.

"Come on, sister, keep up!" Thorn called.

Vision had been too distracted to realize that she was falling behind. She ran after her brother, twisting and turning around the trees and the undergrowth. Racing through the forest kept them fit and strong.

At last, they both stopped, panting hard. Thorn plopped to the ground. Vision sat across from him. The wind blew harder.

"I need to talk to you about something," Thorn said after he recovered his breath.

Vision pricked her ears forward.

His eyes had a mischievous sparkle. "Phase has been sneaking looks at you more often. I think he's showing some interest in you. If you know what I mean. You've been sneaking some looks at him, too."

Vision felt the heat of embarrassment. She had taken an interest in Phase. "I don't think my love life is your business."

"You're my little sister, and it's my job to watch out for you." His tone changed from teasing to serious. "If you don't have any interest in him and he bothers you, I'd like to know about it."

"Don't worry. I can take care of myself." Vision stood.

Thorn meant well, and although it was annoying, she would protect him in the same way in a heartbeat.

A strong gust of wind made her stagger. The air was hot and humid. "Let's go to the river."

Without waiting for Thorn, she shot off into the forest. As she rounded a tree, something caught her attention.

A tall, brown elk with long horns stared at her. The light shone brighter behind him, and the sight mesmerized her. Every time the bull moved his hooves, there were loud crackles. It was odd for him to make that much noise and not run from her. She also couldn't pick up his scent. Something wasn't right.

There was more crackling and snapping and a groaning noise. Something slammed into her side, and teeth closed on her scruff. She thought the elk had charged her, but then she realized it was her brother.

Vision and Thorn tumbled over each other. The noises grew louder, and the ground shook. She scrambled to her feet and looked back at where she'd been standing. An apple tree lay on the ground. It must have fallen. The elk was gone.

"Were you blind and deaf?" Thorn growled. His fur was bristled up with anger, but his eyes were wide with fear. "If I hadn't caught up to you when I did..."

"I don't know. I guess I was distracted," Vision said.

She walked around the fallen tree. There was no scent, footprints, or any sign of an elk. That couldn't be right.

"Thorn, was there an elk standing here?"

"I don't know," he said. "I was too busy trying to make sure that you weren't crushed. We need to tell Mother and Father that some of the trees may fall in this wind. I guess because of the drought."

Vision stared at where she'd been standing. The gravity of the situation sank in. She should've noticed the tree falling. How could she make a mistake like that? What was going on with her today?

"Are you all right?" Thorn asked.

Vision wasn't sure how she felt. "I just want to get away from here."

"Do you still want to go to the river? Or back to the dens?"

"I want to go to the river."

With one more look at the fallen tree, she left with her brother.

Vision thought the incident with the apple tree was just a strange occurrence. Maybe she had been daydreaming and had a lapse of attention. But the hallucinations continued. The disconnects followed soon after.

She had no idea what was wrong at that time, and it scared her. Vision assumed it was mental illness, even though she hadn't heard of her struggles before. She only knew about anxiety, depression, and two or three others.

A couple of months after the first hallucination, a wolf named Oak became very sick. He looked off in a direction and called out to his mate, who had died a few years ago, as if she were there.

Vision's father said that Oak was hallucinating. She asked what he meant, and he told her it was seeing things that weren't real. Vision could then put a name to half of her problems.

Both of the issues didn't happen frequently in the beginning, and she was able to live with them. They worsened as time went on.

Vision was reluctant to ask someone about the issues or even talk about them. What if she was treated like she was weird or crazy? What if her family and friends no longer wanted to be around her and stopped loving her?

It would hurt worse than dealing with the mental illness alone. To be in the pack, yet feel as though she had been exiled, would make her like nothing more than a hallucination. She'd kept silent about her issues for eight years and would probably continue to do so as long as she could get away with it. So far, it seemed as if she had been successful in not tipping anyone off that something was wrong with her, and even that was difficult sometimes.

Vision wandered away from the fallen tree. Right now, they were in another drought. With narrowed eyes, she glanced up and around at the trees. Her ears were pricked, and she kept alert for any hint that one was about to crash down on her, even though the wind only blew gently.

She willed her mind to not play tricks on her. Vision detected nothing but the usual sights and sounds of her forest home. Everything seemed safe for now.

"Vision!" an excited voice called. Phase was home.

Vision wasn't sure if she should be glad or annoyed. She didn't want to deal with anyone right now.

Phase bounded up to her and nuzzled her. Vision returned the nuzzle less enthusiastically.

"Did you catch the robber?" she asked, trying to sound more eager than she felt.

"Yes. The farmer was easily convinced to avoid the alley, and then I worked with the village guard. They sent one of the guards as bait. You can imagine the robber's shock when he realized who he was dealing with. How did your mission go?"

"Not quite as planned." Vision scrambled to figure out what to say. "There was some interference."

"Well, sometimes that happens. Don't let it bother you."

Vision nodded.

An uncomfortable silence stretched between them. Normally, Vision would ask to hear more about Phase's mission. Then he would puff out his chest and regale her with all the details, probably exaggerating some. He took great pride in being a seer wolf. Right now, she didn't have the energy to care.

"Would you like to go hunting before the heat gets worse?" Phase asked. "I'm starving."

He must have picked up on the tension. She might feel more in the mood later to hear about his mission.

Vision figured that spending time with Phase would be better than sulking. But she would let him take the lead in the hunt so she wouldn't point him toward imaginary prey. "Sounds good to me."

SEVEN

T WO AND A HALF weeks later, it was time for the next full-moon ceremony. Vision had been dreading it. The hallucinations and the disconnects had continued at least once every day.

As she walked through the forest next to Phase, her skin crawled. Her head and tail were down, and she dragged her feet. In contrast, Phase held his head and tail up high, and he pranced.

"I can't wait to see what my next mission is," he said. "The last one was so fun."

"Yeah," Vision said glumly. "I'm wondering what I will see, too."

"Don't let your last mission beat you down. You always get another chance. That's what's so great about being a seer wolf."

They settled down at the glade and both gazed up at the moon. Vision waited to see something. She waited and waited. Disappointment filled her, and she looked back down.

After her last failure, maybe the powers that gave them visions thought she didn't deserve another chance. Not having one wasn't unusual, but what if it never happened again?

Vision glanced at the other wolves. Some were still transfixed, and others stared thoughtfully into the distance. Phase was still focused on the moon with his ears pricked forward.

Vision turned her head to the right, and suddenly, the whole forest was ablaze around her. The heat from the fire scorched her fur and skin. Smoky air burned her nose and mouth, and her eyes watered. In the distance, there were shapes in the fire.

She squinted. The shapes looked like shadowy silhouettes of wolves with glowing eyes. A little group was trapped in a ring of flames. She couldn't tell how many there were. The wolves huddled together. One stood at the edge of the group and stared straight at Vision. A tree fell onto the wolves and engulfed the area in flames.

As quick as the sight had appeared, it vanished. Vision's eyes darted around, and her heart raced. The forest was dark, quiet, and peaceful again. The smoky scent and the heat were gone.

Had that been a vision or a hallucination? She wasn't looking at the moon when it happened. What she saw had been clear, but she also felt so confused and anxious. Visions could cause physical sensations, but she'd never felt something touch her or tasted anything in a hallucination before. This would be the first time if it was.

She trembled.

Vision scratched each front paw across the ground. It seemed as though she was connected to reality. She tried to calm down and eventually felt better. Phase shifted next to her. He was done with whatever he had seen.

Phase turned to her. "What did you see this time?"

Vision hesitated. The fire might have just been a hallucination. "Nothing. What about you?"

"I saw a child who wanders off and gets lost. He ends up falling into a deep lake and drowns. I need to find him before he falls and lead him back home. Do you want to come with me?"

"I want to stay home. I'll come with you another time."

Vision was glad she didn't have to travel anywhere this month. She also didn't understand what she'd seen.

Had the fire been a vision or not? She wasn't even sure if the forest she saw was supposed to be Lythannen or somewhere else.

But if it was real, how was she supposed to save wolves from a fire?

EIGHT

V ISION LAY OUTSIDE THE den. She had said
goodbye to Phase earlier. Now, she wondered
what her plans for the day would be.

A voice called her name. Vision glanced around.
No one was looking at her or coming up to
her. It didn't happen again. She wasn't sure she'd
recognized the voice.

Then her father trotted over to her. "Vision, do
you want to go on the keep patrol with me?"

She stood and shook off. "All right."

Whatever she'd heard hadn't been her father's
voice. It was a hallucination. The keep patrol
should be an easy enough activity, and it might
distract her from thinking about the mental illness.

Once a week, two or three wolves were sent
to check on the sorcerer's keep and the weeping
willow tree. The seer wolves had kept watch on the
old outpost ever since the sorcerer had been killed.
They wanted to make sure that no curious people
meddled with something they didn't understand
and that no other sorcerers tried to take up
residence.

They also checked the weeping willow to ensure that no one had messed with it. It was especially important now because the tree was blooming.

A few months had passed since Vision had gone on a keep patrol. She and her father trotted toward the western part of Lythannen. They slowed their pace as the trees and the undergrowth became thicker.

"Tread quietly," her father whispered. "The last patrol said the wierllings are more active again."

After a phoenix named Landa killed one over four months ago, the wierllings had been warier and stayed in hiding. They must finally be brave enough to move around again.

Vision and her father stepped as lightly as they could and used thick brush for cover. They stayed close to each other and focused on their surroundings. Vision was mindful of the grass, dirt, and rocks under her paws, to remain in reality, so she wouldn't pay too much attention to the deeper shadows.

This part of Lythannen was overgrown and gloomy. Vision ducked under a low-hanging vine. More of them grew here, and they tended to be thicker in this part of the forest. One advantage of the dense foliage was that it kept the area underneath it cool in hot weather.

The stillness around them was unnatural. Birds and other animals only moved around occasionally. Every step sounded louder than it should.

There was no set trail because the seer wolves didn't go through enough to create one, and they didn't want the wierllings to be able to predict their movements, just to be safe. They knew the general direction to go. The wolves also always picked a different day each week to do the patrol.

Vision and her father traveled for a while with no trouble. She took in a deeper breath and froze. A smoky, sour scent flooded in. Her father stopped and sniffed the air. A sparrow let out an alarm call, and then nothing else stirred.

A wierlling was close.

Her father ducked into some bushes. She followed and lay next to him. A few moments later, there were soft steps, and a wierlling passed by. All she could see were black boots and the edges of tattered, shabby, black robes.

Vision's heart pounded. She trembled as chills ran through her. She lay as still as she could. Even though she had mental illness, she was glad the wierlling wouldn't sense it and attack her.

She relaxed when the wierlling moved on without seeming to know that seer wolves were nearby. Vision waited for her father to decide when it was safe to keep going. She didn't trust herself to make the right call.

The occasional rustling and noises of other animals and insects began again. Her father slowly stood and looked around. He nodded to her, and they continued on more carefully.

Vision felt more like prey sneaking around to avoid getting eaten. When they reached the tree line, sunlight and fresh, open air washed over her.

Her father stopped and glanced around. "Do you sense any more wierllings?"

Vision couldn't mess this up. She looked around, listened, and sniffed the air. There were no obvious signs of danger.

"No," she said.

"Let's go then."

Vision and her father ran across the clearing. They stopped inside the bottom level of the central tower. This was the only access point to the whole keep. They checked the stone floor, the walls, and the doorways for any suspicious scents.

After they finished, her father gestured toward the staircase with his nose. "Go look up there. I'll check the side towers."

"Yes, Father."

Vision climbed up the stairs. She poked her head into each room and sniffed. They were old, decrepit, and musty, as usual. Nothing looked tampered with.

The trapdoor at the top was securely shut. Vision hadn't found anything out of the ordinary. She turned around. There was a noise like a stone falling down a few steps. She froze and pricked her ears up. Then it sounded as if something was walking up the stairs. She sniffed but couldn't detect a scent.

"Father?"

The noises stopped.

Vision closed her eyes and took a breath. "Everything is okay. It was nothing. You're the only one here."

She opened her eyes. A wierlling loomed over her. The evil creature looked like an animal that had been left to rot and decay. Peering into its eyes was like staring into dark abysses of death.

"No, no." Vision backed up. "Father!"

She kept stepping back until her rump hit the wall, and she collapsed. She thought wierllings didn't come into the keep.

Her heart raced. She curled her lips back and tried to growl, but it came out more like a whimper. Trembling uncontrollably, she pushed herself closer against the wall. There was no room to run past the creature.

The wierlling lunged at her. Vision yelped, shut her eyes, and covered her face with her paws. She tensed as she expected to be grabbed and her life to end. Nothing happened.

She opened one eye and peeked over a paw. The wierlling had gone. This didn't make sense. Vision jumped when she heard a squeak. A mouse stared quizzically at her.

"I don't suppose you saw a wierlling, did you?" she asked the little creature.

The mouse squeaked again and jumped down onto the next step. There were more footsteps.

"Not again," she whimpered as her heart rate picked up.

"Vision, are you up here?"

She relaxed. It was just her father. Vision stood and tried to look less panicked. Now that she thought about it, there was no wierlling scent. It had been another hallucination.

She was now up to two for the day. Vision shook off. Why couldn't her problems stop torturing her for a little while?

Her father rounded the curve of the staircase. "There you are." The mouse scurried past his feet, and he tilted his head. "That's strange."

"What's wrong?" Vision asked.

"We never see any animals like mice or bugs in here. It was assumed that the sorcerer used spells called wards to keep them out. Maybe they're failing. But I don't understand everything about how the humans' magic works."

That brought up a troubling thought. "Would there be wards keeping the wierllings away? Is that why they don't come in here?"

"I don't know. We'll need to monitor the situation carefully. Anyway, is everything all clear?"

"As far as I can tell."

"Let's check the tree and then go back to the dens."

Vision hadn't technically failed at anything so far, but she was more than ready to leave. They started down the stairs. She glanced at the top room as she passed by.

"Father, wait. Something doesn't look right."

She hadn't noticed it earlier, but now that she was looking from higher up, she could see the tops of the tables in the room better. She went in and jumped up to put her front paws on one of them. This time, she was sure she wasn't hallucinating. There were clear areas in the dust where objects used to sit. And the spots were still fairly clean, so it had happened recently.

Her father jumped up next to her. "Someone has been in here. Check again for a scent. What else is missing?"

Vision and her father sniffed around thoroughly, but if there was any scent, it was gone. Now that they were looking harder, they realized that a few items were missing from the bookcase shelves, but some were too high to see, even when they stood on the chairs.

Vision managed to pull open the bottom cabinet doors but had no idea what was supposed to be inside. She saw a few dead moths on the floor. Bugs were getting in here, too.

They both checked in and around the rest of the keep, but found no tracks or traces of the thief. Nothing else seemed to be missing.

"That was a good catch, Vision," her father said. "We need to increase patrols here and check everything more thoroughly. We've grown too lax. I'm surprised the thief didn't take the skulls and that black cloth. They're probably the most powerful objects."

People normally didn't try to steal stuff because the seer wolves and the phoenixes kept a close eye on the keep. Most wouldn't risk trying to make it past the wierllings. This was an odd turn of events.

Vision and her father went down the path leading to the weeping willow. It was easier than trudging through the forest, but they were more watchful for any signs of wierllings. She tried to stay focused, but she flinched at any sound and couldn't let go of the tension in her body.

Hallucinating now would be dangerous. If she couldn't distinguish a real wierlling from a fake one, she or her father could get hurt or killed. What if this happened at or near the dens? Wierllings stayed away from the den sites, but that was never a guarantee.

"Calm down, Vision. I don't think there's anyone here now besides the wierllings," her father said.

Vision tried to settle down.

They reached the tree. The clearing around the weeping willow was the brightest and most beautiful spot in this part of Lythannen that they knew of. After the outpost had been built, this area was going to be used for a second smaller one. The project was abruptly abandoned after the phoenixes negotiated peace among the kingdoms and helped give Lythannen to the seer wolves.

The weeping willow was the final tree to be cut down but was left alone. The sorcerer enchanted it to produce magic purple roses that had healing properties. A few months ago, a rose was successfully used as an antidote to save King Garne of Torrannon when he was poisoned.

Vision looked at the tree with interest. Most of the scorched parts had healed, and the roses bloomed lower down. She picked up a pleasantly sweet scent from just standing near them.

The sorcerer who'd enchanted the weeping willow might have been evil, but this was one piece of magic he'd conjured that seemed light and good.

She wondered how long the roses would bloom. No one could remember when they first appeared.

Her mother wasn't sure what to do with the tree now that it was blooming again. The roses had proven to have healing powers, but it was risky to travel here.

Also, there was the issue of whether to let people cross their borders. The seer wolves couldn't deter trespassers in the western reaches, but they didn't want their territory to be taken over by the humans. For now, the tree was kept a secret from everyone outside of Lythannen, besides the phoenixes and a select few humans.

The seer wolves had tried the roses a couple of times, but they didn't want to constantly come here unless the need was great enough. They didn't know if the flowers would heal everything or if they were less effective for wolves because they were designed for humans. And they were only for physical ailments, so a magic rose wouldn't heal Vision's mental illness.

She sensed something else. There was more birdsong than normal. Dragonflies zoomed around the clearing, and a few butterflies landed on the roses and the wildflowers. A squirrel jumped confidently from one tree to another, seemingly unconcerned about anything. The forest had changed around the weeping willow.

"Father, is it just me, or is this area livelier?"

Her father walked over to the edge of the clearing. "I noticed that. The reawakened magic must be having an effect on the area around it. I wonder if it would keep the wierllings away and how far it extends." His tail wagged.

Crows cawed alarm calls near the path behind them. Vision left her spot by the tree and joined her father. He gestured toward the forest with his nose. It was time to go. Now wasn't the time to test if a wierlling would come near when it was just the two of them.

They headed back through the forest. It was quieter again as they neared the river. After a careful trek, they safely made it back to the dens.

NINE

AN OWL SCREECHED. VISION snapped awake. She had only been dozing. Everyone else in the den was fast asleep.

Vision closed her eyes and tried to relax, but she couldn't drop off to sleep. Her mind spun. If she was awake for too much longer, she would have to nap more during the day so she wouldn't be exhausted and end up having more hallucinations and disconnects than usual.

She stood and stepped over Thorn. Because the older wolves slept at the back of the den and the younger ones closer to the entrance, she didn't have to worry about creeping by several of her denmates. She sat at the entrance.

It was cool and windy tonight. Vision glanced around at the forest and tried to not pay too much attention to the sights that tried to trick her.

She sighed and dropped her gaze to the ground. What was she going to do? She struggled to hunt, she couldn't trust herself to successfully complete missions, and now she couldn't do a keep patrol. How was she going to be a productive member of the pack?

"Can't sleep?" Her mother was lying on the rock formation.

"I guess not," Vision said.

"Come up here with me."

Vision leaped up the hill and lay on the rock next to her mother. She could just make out Raindrop on the other side of the clearing. The she-wolf had white fur with black patches on her back.

Two more guards watched the other den sites somewhere in the shadows. They would switch with three others halfway through the night. Vision was due for night-watch duty soon.

When she had to do it, she struggled to keep her issues in check. Vision was usually exhausted by the time she could go to sleep. She was just happy that all her nights had remained quiet. The last thing she wanted to do was miss a threat to her pack when she shouldn't have.

"Everything is so peaceful," her mother said.

Owls hooted, crickets chirped, and the trees rustled softly in the wind. The sky was clear, so moonlight and starlight glowed down on the forest. There was a comforting tranquility.

"I like that better than the threats we've faced recently," Vision said.

Her mother had a far-off look. "It's the unknown threats that concern me more."

Vision cocked her head. "What are you talking about?"

Her mother stood with a worried look on her face. "Walk with me."

Vision followed her mother as she confidently strode through the forest. She spotted something out of the corner of her eye. A shape had looked human, but it was just a tree. Everything felt real, so she didn't worry about it.

She slowed down when they reached the river, but her mother kept going. It was just the two of them wandering around at night. Her mother stopped in the middle of the river and looked back.

Vision couldn't sense any wierllings. Her mother would be depending on her to be watchful. Vision took another moment to make sure everything seemed safe and then caught up. They crossed the river and went all the way to the full-moon-ceremony glade.

"The missing items from the sorcerer's keep worry me." Her mother sat. "That place is well stocked with magical items and ingredients, but no one has tried to steal anything from it until now. Who took them and why? Where are they now, and what exactly is their plan? After we averted war in Torrannon, Landaro told me that, although he was concerned about the threats that have happened recently, he hoped they would end there. I was hopeful, too. What you and your father found at the sorcerer's keep has done nothing but make me suspicious. Something is not right, and I don't need a vision from the full moon to tell me this. I just don't know what it is yet. We'll all need to be vigilant."

Vision shifted uncomfortably. Could she protect her pack even with her issues? Night watches made her nervous enough.

Her mother's expression softened. "I'm sorry. I didn't mean to frighten you. I'm still trying to figure out a way to tell the pack without causing any panic."

"It's okay, Mother," Vision said.

"The seer wolves have survived many storms and hardships. I believe we will endure whatever else that comes. But we can never forget that, although we play an important role in this world, we also have a duty to protect each other, even if only one wolf howls for help alone. That's how we'll survive."

Vision had heard those words many times before. She wished there was a way someone could help her with the mental illness.

Her mother turned to her with a curious expression. "When you were at the weeping willow, did the forest really feel livelier?"

Vision and her father had mentioned that after they returned from the patrol, but it hadn't been discussed further.

"Something was different," Vision said. "I could sense more life, and it didn't have that eerie stillness we are so used to."

"I've been thinking about that, too. I'm sure your father has it on his mind. He's probably going to want to discuss us hunting in that part of the forest. I wouldn't be surprised if he's making a plan right now. He and Arrow had their heads together, discussing something intently this evening. I don't know if it's worth the risk."

After the incident with the sorcerer and the wierllings, the seer wolves feared that the western reaches of Lythannen might be lost forever. Some of them hoped that if the phoenixes could kill all the wierllings, they could regain their entire territory. Others were skeptical, considering how few had been destroyed so far.

The weeping willow's positive effect on the forest around it was a surprise. The seer wolves had survived even the harshest seasons with their current territory, but a larger area would mean they wouldn't have to hunt in the same places all the time.

But this wasn't a decision Vision could easily help with. She was once again reminded of how her mother carried the heaviest burden in the pack by being the leader—a burden she was glad she didn't have to worry about for now. Her mother was responsible for making sure everyone, from the oldest wolf to the youngest pup, didn't go hungry or thirsty and were well cared for when they were sick or injured. Her top priority was the safety and well-being of the pack.

Vision had some lessons a few years ago about being the pack leader and paid attention to what she needed to know. That was all she hoped she ever had to do.

She also had no desire to hunt close to the sorcerer's keep. Years ago, she would've been excited about it, but now, she dreaded the thought of having to focus on hunting while trying to not have every shadow and noise turn into a hallucination of a wierlling.

Both of them were quiet then. Vision lost herself in her own thoughts. She looked at the spot where she'd seen the fire. Nothing had happened so far. Maybe it had been a hallucination.

"Hunter said you were more uneasy on the keep patrol than usual," her mother said. "You know you can tell me if something is bothering you."

"I'm okay," Vision said. "I was feeling off that day, and I don't like being near the sorcerer's keep."

Her mother nodded. "Well, let's head back and both try to get some sleep." She looked up at the moon. "I hope we'll be granted foresight if some new danger is coming."

TEN

V ISION FOLLOWED AT THE rear of the hunting party. A wounded male deer had been spotted not too far from the dens. It was the middle of the afternoon and still hot, but the wolves wanted to get this done now before their prey tried to wander off. Her father led the group of ten wolves. One of Vision's closest friends, Brook, walked next to her with her pups, Midnight and River, in tow.

Brook had brown fur and brown eyes. Midnight had black fur and yellow eyes, and River had gray fur and blue eyes.

"Remember, girls," Brook said to her pups, "stay with Vision. Bucks have sharp horns and hard hooves. It will most likely put up a fight. Your father and I don't want you two to get hurt."

The pups were too young to join in, but they could watch and learn. Vision had agreed to stay back and keep an eye on them.

They eventually found the deer. He lay in a small clearing and turned his head as the hunting party approached. The buck struggled to stand. His left back leg looked broken.

Vision sat at the edge of the clearing. She made sure Midnight and River settled down next to her. Their tails wagged excitedly. She happily remembered simpler times when it was so neat to watch the adults hunt, hoping that soon she would be big and strong enough to join them.

"Watch closely," Vision said to the pups. "Everyone will have to work as a team and stay on their toes."

Some of the wolves darted in front of the deer's head to distract him and tire him out. Brook just skirted by as he swung his antlers at her. The others positioned themselves to jump on him from behind.

Vision became mesmerized. Her body hummed with excitement. She still felt the thrill of the hunt, even though she just watched. She kept making sure that the pups stayed next to her.

Then she disconnected. Everything looked out of place. The forest blurred. Her packmates and the buck didn't seem real. Vision closed her eyes and shook her head. She snapped back to reality when Brook's mate, Timber, who had reddish-brown fur and golden eyes, let out a triumphant bark.

The hunting party successfully took down the deer. Vision shook her head again. That disconnect had been intense. She checked on the pups, but they weren't there. Their scent led back into the forest.

"Midnight, River," she called and followed their trail. They couldn't have gone far.

Vision could not believe that she'd allowed herself to become so distracted. She would've been able to stop them from leaving if it hadn't been for the disconnect.

She finally heard excited yipping. Vision came upon the pups darting around a raccoon, but something wasn't right. She picked up a particular sour smell emanating from the animal. It hissed and lunged wildly, its coordination all off, and its jaws had foam around them.

"Midnight! River! Get away from the raccoon!"

The pups flinched and put their ears back. They slunk over to Vision with their heads and tails lowered. Vision kept an eye on the raccoon to make sure it didn't try to attack them, but it stayed put. The animal looked dazed.

She softened her voice even as her heart pounded. "Did either of you touch the raccoon?"

"No," both pups said.

"You're absolutely sure?"

"Yes, Vision," Midnight said.

River nodded.

Vision almost sank to the ground in relief.

"We were just practicing hunting," River said.

"Do you see how the raccoon is acting?" Vision asked. "We never mess with animals that show clear signs of rabies."

Both of the pups widened their eyes.

"Father told us about rabies," Midnight said in a frightened voice. "I'm sorry, Vision. We forgot."

"I know. You both got excited and weren't thinking. But this is why, for your own safety, you don't wander off to hunt like this without an adult," Vision said firmly. "Do you understand that?"

"Yes, Vision," they both said.

Something moved through the forest behind them. Brook and Timber ran up.

"We wondered where you went," Brook said.

Vision indicated the raccoon with her nose. "The pups decided to go off on their own hunt."

Brook gave her pups a stern stare. "I thought I told you two to stay with Vision."

Timber went closer to the raccoon but jumped away when it lunged at him. He snapped his head toward them with a panicked look after he must have come to the same conclusion that Vision had.

"It didn't touch them," she said quickly, knowing what his question would be.

"The raccoon has rabies?" Brook asked, her eyes wide.

"Most likely."

"I'm glad you got them away from it." Brook and Timber licked their pups and nuzzled them.

Everything could have turned out much differently. If the disconnect had delayed Vision any longer, she could've been too late. If the raccoon had bitten one or both of the pups, they would've died horrible deaths.

Rabies was rare but had no cure. That's why the wolves carefully assessed animals that looked sick. Dead ones with rabies had the same sour smell. There was also no guarantee that one of the magic roses would heal them.

"I'm sorry," Vision said. "I was distracted, and they got away from me."

"Don't worry," Brook said. "They've slipped away from me and Timber before. The most important thing is that you got to them in time and everyone is okay."

Timber looked back at the raccoon. "I think it died." The animal was still with its mouth hanging open. "We need to tell Hunter. We'll need to get rid of the body when we're sure it's dead."

When a rabid animal died, and it was small enough to be moved safely, the wolves would dig a hole and use sticks to push the body into it to bury it. That way, no other curious pups or animals would be put in danger.

"Let's find the hunting party," Brook said.

Vision sat. "I'll stay and make sure the raccoon doesn't go anywhere."

"Okay. We'll be right back."

She had finally gone and done it. Midnight and River might have been doomed to die. Vision lay down before she collapsed. Her stomach churned, and her chest tightened. She was so mad at herself.

Her friends forgave her, but she couldn't forgive herself for what almost happened. When she had pups of her own, what if she caused something horrible to happen to them? Or she could put the whole pack in danger.

Did she deserve a place here?

ELEVEN

IN THE DEN, VISION snapped awake with the bitter tang of smoke in her nose and her mouth. Was the forest on fire? She turned over and looked out the entrance in a panic.

Everything seemed peaceful. She couldn't remember what she had dreamed about or if she even had. There were no strange scents, so she must have imagined the smoke.

She once again wondered if she should tell someone about the vision. It wasn't necessary. Involving other wolves could change the circumstances of the vision for the worse and put others in danger who didn't need to be. She could also cause panic for no reason. The mission was ultimately hers and hers alone.

Vision sighed and lay back down. She didn't feel like getting up yet. Who knew what trouble she might bring to the pack today?

There were paw steps close by, and she picked up the scents of her parents. Vision pretended to be asleep. They seemed to stop at the entrance of the den. There was a flutter of feathers.

"Hello, Nimbus," her mother said.

Nimbus was a phoenix. He had orange-and-yellow speckles on the backs of his wings, if Vision remembered correctly. The phoenixes regularly visited the seer wolves to exchange news and information. She pricked her ears up. It would be good to pay attention to the conversation.

"Hello, Haven, Hunter," Nimbus greeted.

"I hope you are bringing good news," her mother said.

"Well..." the phoenix hesitated. "Everything is still peaceful. There are no indications that war will break out. Rodrick has made no more invasion attempts. Landaro is concerned that he's missing something, though. The unsolved mystery of who has been harming the royal family in Torrannon is still on his mind."

"I don't have any news that will reassure him. Hunter and Vision discovered that some items in the sorcerer's keep were missing. I've temporarily increased patrols to twice a week."

"Do you know which items?" Nimbus had worry in his voice.

"Books and magical ingredients, from what we can figure out, but we can't see all the places in the keep. Everything else has been peaceful otherwise, but I'm worried about who snuck over there and why. I sent a patrol to check the path, but they couldn't find any clues that would help identify the thief."

"Did you ask any of the people or the guards in the nearby villages?"

"I didn't want to tip off the thief that we know things are missing. If it happens again, we'll have no choice but to ask around."

"This is troubling. Landaro may want to send extra patrols out there, too. I'm sure someone will let you know soon. I need to return to Ehckrist."

They said their goodbyes, but Vision's parents didn't leave yet.

"Haven, there's something we need to discuss," her father said.

"If you're going to ask me about hunting around the weeping willow, I'm not sure if I can give the idea my blessing. We still hold more than half of Lythannen. It's safe, for the most part, and has sustained us for a long time. We barely know that part of the forest anymore. I don't like the thought of sending wolves into potentially dangerous territory."

"But the pack is growing. We'll need more hunting grounds. The magic from the weeping willow might keep the area devoid of wierllings, and it could grow stronger as the tree heals. We've always dreamed of retaking the entire forest. Why not start with the section around the weeping willow?"

"You know very well why I'm cautious about being near the sorcerer's keep." There was a tremble in her mother's voice.

She had been the pack leader for about fifteen years. A wierlling killed Haven's father, Aspen. He was on a keep patrol, and they spotted children on the path who didn't believe the stories about the wierllings and wanted to see the sorcerer's keep.

A wierlling attacked one of the children, and Aspen gave his life to defend them. His mate, Moonlight, was so overcome with grief that she couldn't lead the pack. Apparently, she was a shadow of what she used to be. She passed the leadership to her oldest daughter, Haven, and died soon after. Vision never met Moonlight.

"Hunter, the pack is still so few in number. We can't afford any needless deaths right now. We were fortunate that Starling and Dew weren't killed when they got too distracted chasing those rabbits to realize that they'd strayed all the way to the path, even if it was lucky that they caused us to find Princess Aria at the sorcerer's keep. But it's my job now to protect the pack—not chase potentially fruitless and deadly dreams."

"I know. That's why I want to lead a scouting patrol out there first to see if it seems even remotely safe to hunt. At the first sign of trouble, we'll come straight back. I understand that it'll be dangerous. We won't take chances. As the alpha male, it's my job to protect the pack, too. You can trust me with this."

"How many wolves are you thinking about bringing with you?" Her mother still sounded apprehensive.

"At least eight. Plenty to watch each other's backs and not make too much commotion."

"I see you've thought this through," her mother teased. Vision's father was known for being reckless.

"I always think things through." He sounded as though he was pretending to be offended. "You're the one who's fussy."

"I prefer meticulous. I want to see that area of the forest before I make a decision. We'll bring Arrow. Your brother has the best nose in the pack, and I'm sure you two were already making plans. I want Pine to go, too. My sister can keep an eye on things here while we're gone. We need to think this through and not rush."

"Sounds like a plan."

Vision wasn't sure how much good could come from this.

TWELVE

THE SUN WAS HIGH in the sky by the time Vision got up. Most of the wolves were lying around at the dens. She took a step forward and stumbled when two little bundles of fur charged past her.

Midnight and River darted around the clearing with a few other pups. They wrestled and chased each other, hopping over napping packmates. The older wolves didn't seem to mind and watched with amusement.

Pups were a blessing these days as the pack tried to rebuild their former strength—something Vision could have messed up. Midnight and River seemed to have forgotten their scare from yesterday and were as happy and exuberant as ever.

The raccoon had been safely buried and was no longer a threat to anyone.

Brook lay next to Timber in the shade on the opposite side of the clearing. Vision went over to them. Timber was sleeping.

"Brook, can I speak with you?" Vision asked.

"Sure," her friend said. "Come join us."

"Can I speak with you alone?"

"Oh, all right." Brook nudged Timber. He blinked sleepily at her. "Wake up and watch Midnight and River for a bit."

"Okay," Timber said. He yawned and sat up.

"He lost sleep when the girls woke him up early this morning," Brook said as they climbed the hill. "They haven't even taken a nap yet. I wish I still had their endless energy."

Vision led them away from the dens so it would lessen the risk of anyone overhearing them. They went to a sheltered spot surrounded by trees and blackberry bushes—a secret space that they found when they were younger, where they could hide and talk in secret. Vision and Brook crawled in through a hole they had dug under the bushes and struggled to fit in the little space without getting pricked by thorns.

"You know," Brook said, "this was easier when we were smaller. I think the bushes keep growing bigger." She found a spot to lie down, pushed a stone aside with her paw, and stretched her front legs out.

Vision was sure she lay on a few rocks, but she could barely feel them over the prickles of anxiety that stung her whole body. "It seems like it wasn't long ago that we were pups. Now we're adults, and you have a mate and pups of your own."

"I'm glad we grew up in times of peace without having to worry about all the dangers our ancestors faced. So, what is it that you wanted to talk about?"

Vision opened and closed her mouth. The courage she'd plucked up was fading. She swallowed nervously. Her life was spinning out of control. She didn't know what to do or if talking to her friend about the mental illness would help. Would Brook still want to be her friend? She just couldn't keep silent anymore.

Brook pricked her ears forward and cocked her head. "Is something wrong? Is it about what happened yesterday with the raccoon? No one got hurt. There's no need to keep feeling bad about it."

Vision finally forced herself to speak. Brook was one of her closest friends. Vision hoped she would understand. "It's partly that. There's something I need to tell you that I've never told anyone before. I'm nervous about what you'll think."

"You're my packmate, and you're my friend. You can tell me anything," Brook said reassuringly.

Vision shifted so she was more comfortable. She could barely meet her friend's eyes. "For a few years, I've been having hallucinations and disconnects from reality. I guess you could collectively call the issues mental illness. The first hallucination happened while I was playing with my brother when I was a year and a half. I thought I saw an elk, and then a tree almost fell on me. If Thorn didn't push me out of the way as fast as he did, I probably would have died. I lost the pups yesterday because of a disconnect. I was watching you all taking the buck down, and then I thought everything happening in front of me wasn't real. By the time I came back to reality, Midnight and River were gone. I know I sound crazy."

Brook's eyes widened slightly, and her ears pricked forward even more. But only for a moment. "I wasn't expecting you to say that."

Vision was once again impressed by how calm her friend could be. Brook always tried to not let her emotions get the best of her and tended to internalize them instead of outright showing them. This caused others to sometimes struggle to tell what she felt about something.

But Vision had known her since she was a pup. She saw the momentary shock, and now Brook wasn't exuding even a raindrop's worth of anger or revulsion, only compassion and patience.

"Vision, did you expect me to react negatively? Is that why you didn't want to tell me?" Brook asked.

Vision scraped a paw through the dirt. "Yes."

"You know you never have to be afraid to tell me something. How often do the hallucinations and the disconnects happen?"

"They used to not happen all the time, but lately, they're occurring at least once every day." She felt comfortable enough to speak openly now that she knew her friend wasn't rejecting her. "I know a few things that trigger them, but I haven't been able to figure out how to feel when they are going to happen and stop them early. They've gotten worse over time, especially recently. I've had a few incidents while hunting. I failed my last mission because of a hallucination. When I went on a keep patrol with my father, I thought I saw a wierlling right in front of me in the sorcerer's keep, but it wasn't real."

"How difficult is it to snap out of them?"

"It depends on how intense they are. Sometimes, I close my eyes and shake my head. I can run a paw over the ground to feel something real. A sound that catches my attention also helps."

"There are always a few in the pack who have mental illness. There's no need to be ashamed of it."

But currently, no one in the pack had hallucinations or disconnects that she knew of. Vision looked up and tilted her head. What was a horse doing this far in the forest? Why was it staring at her?

"Vision?"

Something touched her paw. Brook had put her paw on top of Vision's.

"Are you seeing something that's not real right now?" her friend asked.

Vision looked back up. The horse was gone. Rationally, she knew that if it was real, Brook would have sensed it. They would have heard it, too.

"I was," Vision said.

Brook looked in the same direction. "What did you see?"

"It doesn't matter. I fear that one day, I won't be able to snap back to reality. It's getting harder to handle the issues. I could put everyone in danger. I wonder if it would be better for me to leave." She nearly choked on the words.

Brook sat up, tense and alert. "Listen, I know this must be hard on you, but you don't have to leave just because you have mental illness."

She'd expected that response, but Vision still needed to say what was on her mind. "What if something happens again like yesterday but worse? I couldn't live with myself if one of my packmates got hurt because of my mental illness."

"Putting the entire pack before yourself shows how much you care about everyone. And you know everyone cares about you. Mental illness won't change that. You're not a danger to us. Don't worry about something that hasn't even happened and may never happen. Please stay and let's try to figure this out. I wouldn't be able to live with myself if you left and then something bad happened to you."

Vision looked at her paws. "I don't know. All of this is so hard to deal with."

"I may not understand everything you're going through, but I want to help you in any way I can. Is it not the duty of each pack member to take care of each other, especially friends? I don't want to see the mental illness put you in danger."

"I wish this was simpler and easier to fix."

Brook lay back down. "Have you thought about telling your parents and your brother?"

"No. Not right now." Admitting it to Brook had been difficult enough.

"Maybe a healer could help?"

"A healer can't cure me. It would probably be pointless."

"Okay," Brook said sympathetically. It was obvious by the worry in her friend's eyes that she didn't like the idea of Vision continuing to keep the mental illness to herself. "You should at least tell

Phase. If you want to be his mate, I wouldn't keep this a secret from him."

"I know. I'm just not certain how he'll take the news."

"I'm sure he won't react badly. In the meantime, even if you can't stop them, let's start by figuring out if you can get more control of the hallucinations and the disconnects."

Vision nodded, even though she was skeptical. "I'll try."

"Make sure to let me know if there's some way I can help."

"Thank you. It means a lot to me that my mental illness doesn't change our friendship."

"You're welcome. There's nothing you can ever do that would make me not love you. I probably need to get back and check that Timber hasn't fallen asleep again." She sat up.

Vision had another thought. It wouldn't hurt to tell Brook about the fire. What she saw was bothering her, and she wanted to tell someone about it. "Brook, do you know if you have to be looking at the moon to have a vision?"

Her friend tilted her head. "No. Why?"

"At the last full-moon ceremony, I saw nothing. Then I looked down, and the forest was on fire. I'm not sure if it was supposed to be Lythannen or somewhere else. A group of wolves was trapped in a ring of flames. But I don't know if it was a vision or a hallucination. Like I said, I wasn't looking at the moon when I saw it."

Brook tilted her head. "Did it feel like a hallucination?"

"I'm not sure. It happened so quickly. The hallucinations make me dizzy and disorientated, depending on how bad they are. I was anxious and confused after I saw the fire. I also felt and tasted things. Those don't happen with hallucinations. But that doesn't mean they won't. The hallucinations started with seeing things and progressed to smelling and hearing later."

Brook flattened her ears a bit with worry. "We should keep an eye on things. The forest is dry. It wouldn't take much to ignite. Do you think you should tell your mother about the vision?"

"She has enough on her mind. I don't want to burden her with this if I don't need to."

They crawled under the blackberry bushes and went back to the dens. Vision was still uncertain about whether she could gain more control of the mental illness. Every past attempt had failed—probably because she frequently chose to try to ignore the issues rather than deal with them.

She was happy her friend still loved her, but based on everything that had been happening, she felt as though she already had two paws out of Lythannen. This was a last desperate act to try to convince herself otherwise. In her heart, Vision knew what her decision would most likely be.

THIRTEEN

"**P**ACK, GATHER!" VISION'S MOTHER called from the rock formation.

Vision and Brook sat next to Timber as he called Midnight and River to them. The rest of the wolves gathered in the clearing and on the hillsides. More than half the pack was still away on missions.

"The forest around the weeping willow has changed. I have just gone there and looked myself. It is lighter and livelier than usual. The magic from the tree is having a positive effect on the forest around it. We couldn't sense any wierllings, so I've made the decision that a scouting patrol can be sent to investigate the area thoroughly. If it seems safe, we can try to hunt there. Hunter will lead the patrol. Arrow, Pine, and Thorn are going with him, and we'd like at least five more to join them. They will leave right now because the weather is nice today."

Vision's stomach knotted up. She would need to make herself scarce. Thorn or her father might ask her to go, and she absolutely did not want to.

Vision stood as the meeting ended. "Brook, I'm going for a walk. I don't want to go with the scouting patrol."

"You always wander off by yourself. Do you want me to come with you?" Brook's ears were slightly back, and she looked tense.

Her friend must still be nervous that Vision might decide to leave, or she was worried about the mental illness. Or it was a combination of the two.

"No. I'll be fine," Vision said as reassuringly as she could.

Brook stood as though she were going to follow, but then Midnight and River distracted her.

Vision climbed up the hill. She did frequently go off by herself. It was a habit that had grown over the past few years because she was often distressed or annoyed by her issues. It was easier to handle the hallucinations and the disconnects on her own, where no one could see her and question her about them.

"Vision!" her brother called.

She reluctantly stopped and allowed him to catch up. So much for leaving quickly enough to avoid being seen.

Thorn bounded up to her and radiated with excitement. "Do you want to join the scouting patrol? It would be like that one time when we were younger, and we went on our own adventure. Except this time there will be more wolves with us."

Vision cocked her head. "You mean the one we almost died going on? We shouldn't have been in that part of the forest by ourselves."

"It was fun, and we made it out all right."

"Whatever you say."

Vision felt an urge to go exploring with her brother, but she would just put the whole patrol in danger. She turned away. "Not this time, Thorn. Let me know how it went when you return."

"Is this about the hallucinations and the disconnects?" Thorn asked.

A cold wave washed over her. She flicked her gaze back at her brother with widened eyes. He had a concerned and knowing look on his face.

"How..." she asked.

"I heard you talking to Brook earlier," he said.

Vision felt numb. "I never sensed you."

"I was downwind and hunting when I saw you sneak into that secret hiding place you think no one else knows about. When I saved you from the falling tree, that's why you asked me if I saw an elk?"

"It was a hallucination, even though I didn't know it at the time. I saw the elk, and I didn't understand why it was just standing there and staring at me. I heard the tree falling, but I didn't comprehend what was actually happening. When the hallucinations continued and the disconnects joined them, I realized something was wrong."

"You said you were thinking about leaving."

Thorn looked so heartbroken that Vision regretted saying it in the first place. "You know my reasons why."

"Even if you're struggling with mental illness, you still deserve to be here. Others in the pack have different kinds of mental illnesses, but that doesn't mean they should all be cast out. You have a place here, and you're not a threat to us. We can find a way to make it work."

Vision felt pride for her brother. He would make a great leader one day.

"Thorn, we're leaving!" their father called.

"You have a scouting patrol to get to," Vision said.

Thorn nuzzled her. "I love you. I always will. I'll see you later, and we can talk more about this?" He pricked his ears up, and his eyes were full of worry. It wasn't a statement; it was a question. Maybe even a plea.

Vision nodded, but she wasn't going to make a promise out loud that she might not be able to keep.

Thorn trotted back toward the dens, but this time his body was slumped. He probably wished he could stay with her.

Vision felt bad for making Brook and her brother worry so much. But this was a decision that she had to make for herself.

FOURTEEN

V ISION PICKED A RANDOM direction, not worrying about following a trail. She wished she could accompany her brother on the scouting patrol. It would be like old times when she didn't have mental illness.

Vision wanted to laugh like a human as she thought about their adventure when they were younger. Actually, she wasn't sure that an almost ill-fated trip into parts of Lythannen, where they had no business being by themselves, qualified as life being simple.

She remembered that day well.

"Thorn, are you sure about this?" Vision asked.

They were on the edge of the western part of the forest.

Her brother had a mischievous glint in his eyes. "It'll be fun. We've explored every nook and cranny of our territory. If we stay closer to the mountains, there shouldn't be as many wierllings back here in the southern edges. They're more interested in humans anyway, so most of them should be closer to the northern border of the forest. They also tend to hang around the sorcerer's keep, which we'll stay away from. We'll be fine."

Vision wondered again if she should have gone along with Thorn. She was just as curious as him to explore new parts of Lythannen, but she didn't want to be reckless.

Her headstrong brother, on the other paw, had no qualms about jumping headfirst into a dangerous situation so long as he thought he had planned enough to be safe. Exactly why her parents always said that Vision was more like her mother and Thorn was more like his father.

She took another look at the part of the forest they were about to enter. The spring foliage was in full bloom, which would make spotting wierllings difficult, although Vision and Thorn would be able to hide better.

They knew what signs to watch out for if one of those evil creatures was close—the forest going silent, feeling a sudden chill, and smelling a sour, smoky odor when there was no smoke around—but they had never experienced them before. And wierllings didn't leave a scent trail.

She was already nervous about going on keep patrols in a little over a year when she turned two. For right now, going into the western area of the forest might be fine as long as they stayed in the back part.

They had been brought to nearby villages a few times to learn about humans, but they still had to wait two months to turn one year old and be able to shadow other wolves on missions. Vision was bored. This could be a fun change of scenery as long as they were careful—something she would have to keep reminding her brother about.

"Okay," Vision said. "But we can't stay too late. We don't need anyone to catch us. And if something feels really wrong, we need to leave."

Thorn nodded. "Deal."

This part of the forest felt wilder and more untamed but with not as much life besides the foliage. They pushed through thick shrubs. Vision winced when brambles poked her sides.

She looked over to the left as they passed an opening in the trees and spotted the Dranfell Mountains. The trees stopped at an area of grassy hills that transitioned into rocky slopes. She marveled at how high the mountains stretched up into the sky. A layer of clouds shrouded the snow-capped peaks. The Dranfell Mountains would be fun to explore, although she would probably never find her way back. It was too bad that no wolves lived there.

The forest was so quiet. The thicker foliage cast more shadows. They went all the way to the edge of the clearing where the magic weeping willow stood.

She would've liked to have seen the tree before lightning struck it. The weeping willow was probably beautiful before. Now, the trunk was blackened, and the branches were bare. The tree was little more than a skeleton. Thorn went farther.

Vision hesitated. "Don't you think we should go back? The weeping willow is our only landmark on this side of the river."

"I want to see the forest behind the tree," Thorn said. "I don't think the patrols ever go farther than this clearing."

Everything had been going fine so far. She hoped they weren't pressing their luck. "Okay. But just a little farther. I don't want to get lost."

She and Thorn kept exploring until they were both panting. This part of the forest was interesting, but Vision was weary of constantly checking her surroundings.

After a little while, Thorn halted. "Let's go back."

They followed their scent trail. Vision hoped they hadn't been away long enough for anyone to worry. They crossed a gully and clambered up some rocks.

They went around three large boulders into a clearing. Thorn sniffed, and then he lowered his tail and looked tense. Vision sniffed, and her worst fears came true.

She couldn't pick up their scent. The undergrowth in front of them looked undisturbed. She wasn't sure if she recognized her surroundings. They must have veered off their scent trail when they climbed the rocks.

She panicked. "Thorn—"

"I know. It's okay. We'll find our scent," he said.

Thorn's tone was reassuring, even though his eyes were wide, and he looked as if he was trying to hide his fear. Seeing her confident brother struggling to not panic frightened her more.

She and Thorn checked around and made enough twists and turns that they ended up back at the three boulders. They couldn't figure out which way was east.

"Where did we go wrong?" Thorn asked no one in particular. He nosed around the other side of the clearing.

Vision sat by the boulders and looked at a patch of flowers next to her. She studied one to try to figure out what they were. The flower was mostly pink. Five petals stuck straight up. The bottom of the flower had a pink striped part that looked like a pouch. A white petal stuck out of the pouch like a tongue that had a yellow patch with pink spots at the top. Another pink petal hung over the top of the pouch.

She'd found orchids they didn't often see. The humans called them calypso orchids or fairy slippers. Vision didn't know who Calypso was or what fairies were supposed to be, but the flowers were beautiful.

A stick broke, and something rustled near her. "Thorn, is that you?"

She trembled. It felt as though something was watching her, and the forest was quieter.

"Vision," her brother called softly. He peered out from under a vine-wrapped spruce tree across from her. His ears lay flat. "Come here, quickly."

Vision slunk over to him. Thorn's tail was half-tucked.

"We have to get out of here. I think there's a wierlling nearby," he whispered. "Follow me. I'm sure I know which direction to go."

They both stayed low. Vision followed her brother closely. They were crossing an open area when there was more rustling near them.

Two wierllings appeared. As though surprised to see seer wolves in this part of their domain, they stopped and took a step back. The wierllings looked terrifying. Vision inhaled the smoky, musty scent and trembled harder as a chill went through her. The forest was silent.

"Run!" Thorn yelled.

Vision ran as fast as she could. She didn't want to lose sight of her brother. She caught her foot on a root but quickly recovered.

Would she be grabbed and pulled back magically at any moment? The wierllings had a magical power called telekinesis, which she didn't want to experience. She couldn't tell if they were being pursued, and she wasn't going to slow down to find out.

They jumped over a fallen log and skirted around a moss-covered rock formation. A gnarled oak tree, with a hole in its trunk, whizzed by as she sprinted past. Thorn kept them going in the same general direction. They ran and ran.

Vision breathed hard, and her legs ached. Relief washed over her when she sensed that they'd crossed back into their own part of the forest. Thorn turned left onto a trail and didn't slow down.

Vision risked a glance back, but she couldn't see anything. She still felt on edge, but it could just be from fear—the wierllings might not follow them this far. Soon enough, she heard the gurgling of the Tam River.

Star, who had blue eyes and black fur with a white patch on her chest, was drinking from the river. She snapped her head up as they rushed across. "What's going on?"

"Wierllings," Thorn said breathlessly. "Two of them. I don't know if they're still chasing us."

Star pricked her ears up. "Go back to the dens, and have a few more wolves sent out here."

Vision checked behind her again. There was nothing.

Vision and Thorn never revealed where exactly they encountered the wierllings. They were both too nervous to sleep that night, afraid that the creatures would come to the dens to find them. Thorn recovered faster and eventually fell asleep. Vision stayed up all night.

After that incident, they were more than happy to stay in the safer areas of the forest unless traveling to the other part was necessary. Thorn's recklessness was also tempered. They learned an important lesson about foolish adventures and needlessly risking their lives.

FIFTEEN

W AS SHE DOING THAT now? Needlessly risking the lives of her packmates? Her heart told her that she was. The hallucinations and the disconnects weren't just going to go away. She didn't know how to control them. Even if she tried, she feared it might be a lost cause.

Vision's foot slipped into a crack in the ground. Almost everything was dried up. She thought back to the fire that she saw at the last full moon. She still didn't know if it had been a hallucination or a warning. What use would she be in saving wolves from a fire anyway? She would probably get them killed.

Vision jumped onto a boulder and looked around. The familiar sights were so beautiful. The scents of her packmates and the forest washed over her. This was her home, but she could be a danger to it. Brook and Thorn saw hope, but Vision could no longer see it. She barely trusted her mind to know what was real anymore.

Something watched her. Vision crouched and sniffed the air. She couldn't smell any of her packmates. There was still plenty of noise, so she was sure it wasn't a wierlling.

She waited and listened. Then she spotted something in the shadow of a mountain laurel shrub. It looked like a raccoon. The shape staggered out into the open with wild eyes and foaming jaws.

It stared straight at her and growled and hissed. She couldn't pick up a scent, though. Vision scraped a paw over the rock. The raccoon disappeared. She sighed.

Despair weighed her down. Now, the hallucinations were mocking her. She couldn't walk through the forest without breaks in reality, and now she had to worry if a rabid animal was real or not. The hallucination had happened with no clear warning or any way to prevent it. She really was broken.

The decision seemed clear. Brook was right about one thing. Vision had a duty to protect her pack. If she couldn't keep herself safe, then she wouldn't be able to keep her packmates safe either. Or raise pups. She didn't belong here.

Vision jumped down from the boulder. The pack would be better off without her. If there was going to be a fire, someone else would be more helpful. She would go someplace where she wouldn't be able to hurt anyone other than herself.

A plan formed in her mind. She would have to look for something to roll around in so she could disguise her scent and not leave a clear trail.

Vision glanced around to make sure she was alone. "I'm sorry, Brook. I wish you and Timber the best. I hope Midnight, River, and any future pups grow up to be strong and brave. I'm sorry, Thorn.

You want to keep me safe, but you can't protect me from my own mind. Mother, Father, I'll never be able to live up to your expectations. I love all of you, and I'm sorry it had to be like this. But leaving will be the best way to protect the pack."

A pang of sorrow hit her, so intense that her chest hurt.

"Phase," she said in a strained voice, "my love, I hope you don't try to find me. It will be better if you move on and pick someone else to be your mate. Please don't live the rest of your life pining for me."

Now was the best time to leave so no one could stop her. And at least she wouldn't have to worry if anyone else would have a negative reaction to her mental illness. It was better to leave and never know than to stay and be rejected.

She basked for one more moment in the familiar sights and smells of her forest home. Then she found the nearest trail.

Vision made sure she knew where it led and that it was real. The trail should take her toward Torrannon. That would be perfect. From there, she would find someplace remote enough that she wouldn't be disturbed.

Perhaps somewhere close to the mountains. That would be nice.

SIXTEEN

F OR ONCE IN A long time, Vision was in control. This was her decision, and it felt right. She moved quickly, determined to go some distance before she disguised her scent.

"Where are you off to?"

Vision froze and turned around. Magnolia stared at her curiously. She had light brown fur and yellow eyes. Magnolia was Haven's sister.

"That trail will lead you straight into the western part of the forest, if you aren't careful," Magnolia said. "And there's a storm coming. I wouldn't want to get caught out there if the weather gets bad."

Now that Magnolia had said it, Vision heard a low rumble. The air was humid and still. Her perfect plan wasn't working out so well. She knew the trail led through the western part of the forest, but she was willing to take the risk.

"What's wrong, Vision?" Magnolia tilted her head. "You look like something's bothering you."

Vision and her brother had a good relationship with Magnolia. She spent a lot of time watching them as pups when their parents were busy.

"I'm okay," Vision said. "I just wasn't paying attention."

"Why don't you come to the river with me? Watching the water always calms me."

Vision wanted to leave now before she lost this opportunity. But she had to be patient for a little while longer. Magnolia might get suspicious if she refused. It wouldn't do any harm to see the Tam River one last time. She could slip away later.

"Okay," she said.

Vision slowed her pace as Magnolia hobbled along next to her. The older wolf broke her right front leg in a hunting accident years ago. The bones hadn't healed properly.

Magnolia had tried a rose from the weeping willow, but it had no effect on her leg, probably because the injury was technically healed. Or the roses really could be less effective on wolves. Magnolia spent most of her time looking after her sick, injured, and elderly packmates. She also took over a lot of the night-watch duties and went on errands for her sister.

The river had receded quite a bit, but the water still flowed. Magnolia found a spot to lie in the shade. Storm clouds were rolling in from the south. Good. They needed the rain.

Vision stared at the water. It didn't give her much comfort.

"I don't plan on staying long," Magnolia said. "I can't just run back to the dens like I used to."

That was fine. Vision cocked her head. "You don't sound disappointed about that."

Magnolia never made a fuss about her leg. Not even after the rose didn't work. Vision would be as devastated about a physical disability as she was about the mental illness.

"I used to feel hopeless," Magnolia said. "Being more dependent on everyone frustrated me and tested my patience, which I didn't have a lot of years ago. I just wanted everything to go back to normal. But I can't change the past. This is how my life is now. And the others love me and value me despite my disability. That's the most important thing. Just because I can't walk as well as the others doesn't mean I don't deserve to be here. I would have destroyed myself if I kept wishing that my leg never broke."

Her words rang hauntingly true to Vision. Would everyone still love her and value her despite all her issues, and was she destroying herself by wishing she didn't have mental illness?

"I would've liked to go with the scouting patrol," Magnolia said wistfully. "I miss hunting and going on missions all the time. It would've been nice if the rose had worked, but I've made peace with my disability. Remember, Vision, whatever obstacles you face in life, have the courage to meet them head-on rather than trying to run away."

Crack!

Vision jumped. A loud clap of thunder followed the lightning strike, and a cool wind picked up. As they watched for a few moments, the sky grew darker and more lightning struck.

Magnolia stood. "I hope the scouting patrol had the good sense to come back or find cover. I think it's time for us to take shelter, as well."

Vision hesitated as Magnolia made her way toward the dens. She needed to make a decision. Leave or stay?

"Vision, are you coming?"

She should make sure Magnolia made it to the dens all right. So no leaving at the moment. Vision went to catch up, but then she wrinkled her nose when she picked up a bitter odor. "Magnolia, do you smell smoke?"

The other wolf sniffed the air. "I do. It's coming from the southwest."

The lightning must have started a fire. The scouting patrol would be somewhere in the same direction. The vision of the fire and the trapped wolves flashed in her mind. The magical instinct kicked in. She needed to go in the direction the smoke was coming from.

What she saw at the full moon wasn't a hallucination. This was her task. Running away now could condemn the scouting patrol to death, including her family. It would be too dangerous for Magnolia to go into a fire, and it would take too long to find someone else and explain. Even then, they wouldn't know where to go.

She had been ready to abandon the mission, but now that she was faced with it, Vision would never be able to live with herself if she stood by and did nothing. Mental illness or not, she had to be brave enough to face the obstacles in front of her.

Vision took a step toward the river. "Magnolia, go back to the dens, and tell my mother that there's a fire. I have reason to believe that the scouting patrol is in danger. I'm going to find them and make sure they get out safely."

Vision sprinted across the river, ignoring Magnolia's calls for her to come back. No more running away. She would prove to herself that she still deserved a place in the pack or die trying.

SEVENTEEN

V ISION FOCUSED ON THE instinct. The smell of smoke grew stronger. Thunder boomed and lightning crackled. She reached the edge of her pack's territory. The instinct was leading her into the western part of the forest.

The storm clouds and the smoke made everything darker and more ominous than usual. Vision closed her eyes and took a few deep breaths. She needed to stay as focused as she could.

She plunged into the forest. Eventually, she saw a light up ahead. The forest was already ablaze. The drought had made everything perfect for a fire.

She had to be careful. The instinct wasn't infallible. If she became confused and distracted, she could lose focus on it. Wandering aimlessly in a fire was too risky. Then she heard something.

The wind carried the sound of desperate howling. The scouting patrol was in trouble. Within the howls, she heard Thorn and her father. They probably hoped their cries would carry to the dens, but Vision doubted they would.

She took a deep breath and answered with a powerful howl of her own. A few moments passed. She listened and heard the scouting patrol again.

Vision ran in the direction of the howls. Now she had a second option to help her pinpoint the scouting patrol if the instinct failed her.

As she went deeper into the fire, Vision skirted by burning trees and brush. She barely avoided a falling branch. The heat building up was worse than a hot summer day.

Then Vision felt a chill. She ducked behind a tree as two wierllings sprinted past. At least the fire scared them. She wouldn't have to worry about those creatures attacking her.

Vision kept moving. Eventually, she was in the thick of the fire. She blinked to clear the tears from her eyes. The smoke made her cough and gag. She stopped. Everything was smoke, flames, and chaos. She could barely feel where the instinct wanted her to go or get a good breath in to howl again.

Suddenly, the fire melded together. The smoke gathered behind the flames. The fire built up like a giant wave. It rose higher and higher, ready to crash down on top of her. Vision couldn't even see the trees or the sky. Voices laughed at her as though they believed she had failed.

Vision tucked her tail and crouched. Did she really think she would be successful at this? She wasn't strong enough to accomplish this mission. Vision let out a whine.

Howls drowned out the mockery. They were long and mournful. The scouting patrol was losing hope.

Vision scraped her front paws over the heated ground. The tang of the smoke stung her nose and her throat. Fire popped and crackled, wind roared, and there were still the occasional sounds of thunder and lightning.

Like waking from a dream, her mind cleared, and the hallucination faded. The voices disappeared. Vision wavered and coughed when she snapped back to reality.

She might not think of herself as strong and heroic, but she had a duty to her packmates, nonetheless. Focusing harder on the howls and the instinct, she shoved everything else out of her mind.

"I hear you. Don't give up. I'm coming."

She pushed on. A burning log blocked her path. She needed to get over it; there was no way around it. The flames suddenly resembled snakes striking and snapping.

"No," Vision growled and shook her head. "Stop it."

The fire returned to normal. Vision backed up, took as deep of a breath as she could, and charged forward. She cleared the flames as she leaped over the log.

Vision went a little farther. Next, a wall of flames blocked her path. Then she saw one open spot under a spruce tree. She crawled through and entered a clearing. Fire blazed all around. The scouting patrol huddled in the middle, their ears flat and their tails tucked.

Her father ran over and greeted her, his eyes wide and full of fear. "Vision, I thought that was you howling. When we didn't hear you again, I was afraid that something bad happened to you."

Thorn also came over and nuzzled her. "Lightning struck ahead of us. We turned around, but it must have struck behind us. We didn't know which way to go to escape."

Vision looked over her shoulder at the spruce tree. It had vines wrapped around it. The tree seemed familiar. She glanced around and saw three large boulders and calypso orchids.

"Thorn, do you remember this clearing?" Vision asked.

"I don't know. You're always the one with the better memory."

She remembered their adventure. From this side, the spruce tree looked impassable because of the flames behind it. She coughed as she crawled under the branches again.

Once the wolves got through, they could follow the direction she and Thorn ran from the wierllings so long ago. It seemed safe. She no longer had the instinct to guide her, but her memory was clear.

She backed out. "I know which way to go."

"Are you sure?" her father asked.

"I am."

"That's good enough for me." Her father looked at the others. "Everyone, follow Vision."

She scrambled back under the branches and led the way. They reached the area where she and Thorn had encountered the wierllings, and she recognized the landmarks from then on. Vision kept a good pace as they passed the fallen log, the moss-covered rock formation, and the gnarled oak tree with a hole in its trunk. Their path kept them away from the worst of the fire.

Vision focused on the memory. A disconnect tried to drag her under, but she concentrated on the steps, panting, and occasional coughing of the wolves around her. Her brother's fur brushed her side. The disconnect faded away.

The air became clearer as they left the fire behind. Soon enough, the wolves made it away from the danger and back to their territory. Some of them collapsed as soon as they reached safety.

Vision gulped in fresh air. She still couldn't believe that she'd saved her packmates despite having hallucinations and a disconnect. Everyone was safe. She'd faced her issues and not allowed them to hold her back.

EIGHTEEN

A WET DROP HIT Vision's nose. The thunder and the lightning had faded a bit. Rain was falling. She hoped the fire would be put out before it became a danger to the seer wolves.

The scouting patrol stumbled to places where they had more shelter, some of them still panting heavily. Vision was ready to flop down and take a nap.

Her father came over and licked the top of her head. "I'm so proud of you. As I escaped, a tree fell, and the whole clearing caught on fire. If you hadn't come when you did, I don't know what would have happened."

Vision hadn't been a moment too soon.

Thorn put a paw over her shoulder. "How did you find us?"

"I had a vision about wolves trapped in a fire at the last full-moon ceremony," she said.

"I assume the instinct guided you to us, but did it direct you back out?"

"No. It was something else. Remember our adventure we went on?" Vision didn't have to look to know her father's eyes were narrowed. "I recognized some of the landmarks that we had gone past when we ran out."

"It was a lucky thing that you did. We rushed out of there so quickly that I didn't pay attention to anything."

"Is there something I need to know about?" her father asked sternly.

"Do you really want us to tell you, Father?" Thorn asked.

He glared at them and then shook his head. "Never mind."

Another group of wolves ran up. Vision's mother was in the lead, and she sprinted over to them. "Is everyone okay?" she asked in a shaky voice.

"Yes," Thorn said. "We were trapped in the fire, but Vision found us and led us out."

Her mother nuzzled her. "You risked your life and saved the patrol. I'm very proud of you."

Some of the other wolves came up to her and thanked her, too. Vision spotted Brook. She went over to her to get away from all the attention.

Brook nuzzled her. "I wasn't sure if I would see you again. I feared that you were going to leave. And then you went and saved the scouting patrol. When you saw the wolves trapped in the fire, it was a vision, after all."

"I did think about leaving," Vision said. "I felt like I had no place here."

"What about now?"

She looked around at her packmates. Vision had been entrusted with the task of saving the scouting patrol, and she'd been successful. If she had left Lythannen, the outcome might have been far worse. She felt at peace with herself for once in a long time.

"I've learned that I need to meet my issues head-on instead of trying to run away from them," Vision said. "I'll stay and figure out how to make this work. I think it's also time to tell some of the others. Can you help me with that?"

Brook nodded. "You know I'm always here for you. And don't worry. They'll understand and love you no matter what. You have a place in the pack, and nothing will change that."

Vision actually allowed herself to believe that.

NINETEEN

W HEN THE RAIN SLOWED to a drizzle, the wolves returned to the dens. Luckily, no one from the scouting patrol was injured. They were just worn out. A couple of wolves stayed behind to make sure the fire didn't spread.

Vision was showered with thanks from her packmates. Delight rushed through her when she spotted Phase bounding up to her.

He had concern in his eyes. "I saw smoke as I arrived back home. What happened?"

"Everything is fine. I'll fill you in," Vision said.

She told Phase what had occurred with some input from Thorn and her father. The rest of the pack listened in closely. She left out the parts about the hallucinations and the disconnect.

Midnight and River ran up to her.

"You saved the wolves from the fire like you saved us," Midnight said.

"You're a hero," River added.

"I just did my duty. Remember, little ones, you must always protect your packmates, even if only one howls for help alone."

A few of the others nodded or voiced their agreement.

Vision was still tired when she woke up from her nap, but it was a good kind of tired. Exhaustion from saving her packmates was better than from the mental illness. She stretched and padded out of the den. Because of the rain, the forest was alive with the croaks of frogs.

The sun was falling. It would be dark soon. The pack was just hanging around the dens. They'd had enough excitement for one day. She sought out Brook.

Her friend pricked her ears up when Vision approached her. Timber was distracted with the pups.

"I'm ready to tell them," Vision said, even though her stomach was in knots. But if she didn't do it now, she might never be ready.

They gathered her parents, Thorn, and Phase. Vision also fetched Magnolia. She led them to a spot away from the dens. Once everyone had sat, she looked at Brook, and her friend nodded.

Vision gathered as much courage as she could. "Thorn and Brook already know what I'm going to say, but the rest of you need to be told. For several years, I've been having issues with mental illness, specifically disconnects from reality and hallucinations. The hallucinations cause me to see, hear, and smell things that aren't real. The disconnects just make everything around me seem unreal. They can make carrying out simple tasks difficult, and they've been worse recently."

"Is that why you were more nervous on the keep patrol than normal?" her father asked.

"Yes. When I went to the top of the keep, I hallucinated that a wierlling attacked me. I was really on edge afterward."

Her mother pricked her ears up. "Why didn't you come to us sooner?"

"I'm ashamed of the issues. When I had the vision about the fire, it happened after I looked away from the moon, so I wasn't sure if it was a real warning or not. I even failed a mission because of a hallucination. I'm afraid that those closest to me will no longer love me because of my mental illness and treat me like I'm crazy. I don't want to feel like an outcast." Vision lowered her head.

Her mother bumped her with her nose. "Just because you have mental illness, it doesn't mean we will stop caring about you. Remember, your ancestor, Omen, had mental illness, yet he was one of the greatest pack leaders we've ever seen. His struggles did not define his place in the pack nor was he loved any less."

"Thank you, Mother. It means a lot to hear that." Vision calmed down. This was going far better than she had expected. She'd heard stories about Omen, but she'd forgotten that he had mental illness. Apparently, even pack leaders didn't need to be in perfect condition to still belong here. "Magnolia, thank you for telling me about your struggles. It really resonated with me and gave me the motivation to confront my own issues."

"You're welcome," Magnolia said. "I was glad to help one of my family members."

Phase moved closer to Vision. "Is there anything we can do to help?"

"I need to figure out if I can predict when the issues happen and stop them early, or prevent them, or at least control them better," Vision said. "I had two hallucinations and a disconnect in the fire, but I tried to stay more focused and snapped out of them quickly. There probably won't be a perfect process for dealing with the mental illness. For now, all I can say is that if it looks like I'm really distracted or distressed, calling my name or touching me can help me break out of it. If I can focus on something real, I can reconnect to reality. I'll try to think of other ways. The hallucinations can also cause me to be dizzy or disorientated. The disconnects only sometimes cause disorientation. Shadows, especially at night, exhaustion, and stress can trigger the issues. Also, I don't need any special treatment from anyone. Just remind me that I'm worthy to be here, even when I doubt it."

"That won't be a problem," her father said.

"We all love you, and we're here to help you," her mother said.

The others nodded in agreement.

"I love all of you, too," Vision said. "I need to speak to Phase about something alone, if you all will excuse us."

As the others left, Brook gave Thorn a shove when he took too long.

"What do you want to talk to me about?" Phase asked.

"A long overdue subject. Phase, I do want to be your mate. I've wanted to for a while. I was hesitant because I didn't know if I would be a good mate and mother with my mental illness or what you would think of me. I was so scared that your feelings about me would no longer be the same once you knew."

To her surprise, Phase beamed with happiness. "Vision, I have always loved you exactly how you are. The mental illness doesn't change anything. You're going to be an amazing mother, and you won't go through everything alone as long as I'm here. I can promise you that."

Warmth spread through her chest, but this time, it wasn't from embarrassment. "I love you, too. I'm excited to move forward instead of avoiding my issues."

TWENTY

A FEW DAYS PASSED. Several rainstorms came through, which put the forest fire out before it could spread any farther. Vision followed another scouting patrol as they went to survey the damage.

Phase walked next to her. Vision's parents, Thorn, Arrow, Pine, and a few others were with them. Her family and friends had been delighted when she announced that she and Phase were mates.

The scouting patrol left their territory and entered the western part of the forest. Vision realized that when she received the warning about the fire, she'd looked in the direction that it happened.

They eventually found where the forest had burned. A bitter scent surrounded them, and as the wolves walked through the ash, it puffed up with each step. They would have to wash off in the river on their way back.

Arrow stopped, his tail and ears drooping. "The forest is gone."

The thick undergrowth was either shriveled up or destroyed. Trees were bare and blackened besides a few patches of leaves here and there.

"Not quite," Pine said. "Just a little scarred."

Vision's mother pushed a fallen branch aside, revealing some green vegetation that the fire hadn't damaged. "Don't think of it as a loss. The forest will heal and be cleansed. If the fire scared the wierllings away, they may not be eager to return. In time, this area may be our hunting grounds once again."

Thorn nudged Vision. "Maybe we can explore it without so much risk. If you want to."

"I'd like that," she said.

While the scouting patrol explored the burnt forest, Vision tried to stay calm and remain more aware of herself so she could maybe feel when the hallucinations and the disconnects would happen. So far, she struggled to find any warning signs, but she kept studying the issues.

She also kept trying to ground herself to prevent them in the first place. It didn't get rid of them entirely, but it already helped to reduce their frequency.

Right now, her efforts were tedious, but now that Vision knew she had others to love and support her, she was motivated to keep trying. She had conceded that if she didn't make any progress by herself, then she'd have to see a healer. Vision also worked on sleeping better and not letting herself get too stressed out. She cared deeply about her pack, but she needed to make sure she took care of herself, too.

The scouting patrol checked on the weeping willow. The fire hadn't reached the tree. Then they went to the edge of the forest on the south side, which just had burnt patches. Vision gazed at the Dranfell Mountains. Curiosity filled her. The mountains looked the same as the ones closer to their territory, but they were new and fascinating at the same time.

Vision turned to Phase. "Do you ever wonder what secrets the Dranfell Mountains hold?"

"I have but I'm content to stay in the forest," he said.

She felt at home in the forest again, too. Fighting to gain control of the hallucinations and the disconnects was going to be difficult, but she felt more confident about handling them. She might have extra obstacles to face than some of the others, but she was ready to meet them and rise above them.

Thank you for reading my story. If it's not too much trouble, I would appreciate it if you left an honest review. Even just one or two lines would suffice. See you in the next story!

Keep reading for a sneak peek of Sparks Shall Rise:
A Stormy Path

CHAPTER ONE

"**H**I, MOM. I HAVEN'T come here to talk to you in a while," Aria said.

She sat on a marble bench in the mausoleum next to the castle where members of the royal family had been interred for generations. The walls and the floor were the same light gray stone as the castle, and the plates covering the tombs were marble with gray veins.

"I brought you some fresh morning glory." Aria put her mom's favorite flowers in the vase attached to the tomb. She pushed her hair back behind her shoulders and took a breath.

Her mom had had long, brown, wavy hair too, although it had been a shade darker than Aria's golden-brown hair. Her eyes had been green. Aria's eyes were hazel.

"I had little time to grieve your death before I fell into health anxiety. Dad's poisoning dredged the memories up, and for the first time in I don't even know how long, I'm allowing myself to deal with it properly. As far as the mental illness, I'm doing better. I'm taking things day by day. My goal is to build myself up stronger than before. However, I'm at a loss with how to achieve it. I only know what I fear. It's hard to move on, and I can't forget everything I read about in those medical books. I had told myself that I didn't want to die, but I don't want to live like this. Don't worry. I'm not suicidal anymore. It got dark during that time, but I'm trying to live a happier life now. It's not always easy. Most of the time, I want to fully relax, but my mind makes me think that I'm giving myself a false sense of security. And then I get more worried. I had so much hope that I could fight this, but I didn't realize how difficult it would be. Dad and Jayce support me, which helps. I wish you were here, though, Mom."

Aria felt tears welling up in her eyes and took a few seconds to get a hold of her emotions. She ran her hands over her thighs and smoothed out the skirt of her blue dress. "No one has found Karl and Everett, despite the price on their heads. Those two and anyone else responsible for your death and the attempted murders of me and Dad have gotten away unpunished. It makes me angry. It's not fair. We watched everyone in the castle for weeks, but it's unclear if Karl and Everett had partners. We still don't know if Rodrick is involved in anything. There's no evidence. It didn't surprise him to see me alive five months ago and otherwise, he didn't act suspicious. We're more careful about who is allowed to work in the castle now. Whether it prevents more trouble, who knows? Well, it's time to go. Dad wants me to help with paperwork. You know how much he hates sitting and sorting through papers, so I'd better go help him. I love you.

I'll talk to you again soon." Aria kissed her fingers and pressed them to the cover of the tomb.

When she stood, sunlight from a window shone on two tombs at the back. One was King Cyrus, an ancestor from long ago. The plate covering his tomb was made of gold, and a likeness of his sword was embossed on it.

His sister, Princess Eleanor, was interred next to him. She also had a gold plate, but hers had a dove holding an olive branch in its beak. Both plates shone brightly when the sunlight hit them just right, making the embossed sunbursts seem to be aflame.

Cyrus was the warrior. Eleanor wanted a peaceful life. Together, they had helped to shape Torrannon into how it was today.

They left a lot to live up to. Aria had had doubts about her ability to be a successful ruler since before she developed anxiety.

She stood with her mom on a balcony and watched stable hands lead a group of new horses for the cavalry through the gate. They had returned from visiting Thangore, a village close to the castle. Her mom had worked as a seamstress there before she became the queen. Interacting with the people brought up feelings of self-doubt for Aria. Her mom seemed to always know what to say and how to act. It looked effortless for her.

Aria still felt awkward at times. She had big shoes to fill when she became the queen. "I don't know how I'll ever be as great of a queen as you, Mom."

Her mom frowned. "Why do you think that, my sweet girl?"

"The people love you, and you make being the queen look so easy. I'm afraid I won't live up to those expectations."

"Oh, Aria." Her mom wrapped an arm around her shoulders. "Don't worry about people comparing us. They already love and respect you, and you still have time to learn. I don't see any reason why you won't be a great queen one day."

Aria smiled. "Thank you."

"And Jayce, that new royal guard, may make an excellent king."

Aria blushed and looked away.

"Don't think I haven't seen how you look at him."

Aria frowned. "He doesn't seem interested, though."

"You two have only known each other for three months. Give it time. If you want my opinion, you should date him if you can. I have a good feeling about him."

"Why do you have a good feeling?"

Her mom grinned. "I learned a long time ago that when the right people come into your life, hold on to them. The wrong people need to be let go of, especially if you see the warning signs. Never fail to heed the warning signs." Her voice faded, and she had a faraway look in her eyes.

"Mom?"

Her mom shook her head. "It's okay. I'll be by your side no matter what happens."

Aria hadn't known at the time all the bad stuff that would happen not too long after that conversation. The loss of her mom, the anxiety, the depression, suicidal ideation. And then her kidnapping and her dad almost being killed. But she had also come a long way as far as feeling much more confident that she could be the queen one day. There was some self-doubt and probably always would be, but it was easier to deal with.

She walked back out of the mausoleum. It was a windy but also hot August afternoon. Last month, they had heard about a fire in Lythannen that was started by lightning. It had been behind the sorcerer's keep but didn't endanger the seer wolves. What a shame it hadn't burned that cursed outpost.

Jayce jumped up from where he was sitting and waiting.

"You know," Aria said, "I could have come here by myself. I carry my knife with me all the time like you and Dad wanted, and I'm doing more fight training."

"We can't be too careful right now, babe. I'd rather know that you're safe, even inside the walls of the castle."

Jayce called her babe now, the term of endearment that she liked best. She used it too, but they said it when they were mostly alone and not having to be professional. Jayce offered his arm, and they followed the path back toward the courtyard arm in arm. The mausoleum was on the right side of the castle.

Wind blew Aria's hair into her face, and she pushed it back the best that she could. She should have braided it. When the mental illness had been worse, she barely had the energy to braid her hair or even put it in a bun. Now, she fixed it up more often.

Aria liked her long hair, although she suppressed jealousy when she looked at Jayce's short, brown hair that was barely being affected by the wind. And the short stubble on his face wouldn't cause any issues, either.

Jayce glanced at her and furrowed his eyebrows. "What?"

"Nothing," Aria said. "I saw you talking to Vivian earlier. Is there still no word about Karl and Everett?"

Jayce shook his head. "They've disappeared."

"You and Vivian get along really well. I didn't know her to play favorites."

Jayce chuckled. "She doesn't play favorites, or I don't think she does. But she and I understand each other."

"How so?" Aria asked.

Jayce opened and closed his mouth and then looked away for a moment. He squeezed her hand. "Sorry, babe. It's not my place to tell. You'd have to ask Vivian."

"She doesn't talk much about herself or her past, even when asked." The forty-one-year-old captain was an enigma. Aria trusted Vivian with her life but knew little about her.

"There is a reason, but like I said, it's not mine to tell. I meant to ask earlier, have you had any other issues with arm pain?"

"I try not to think about it. I'm still having trouble with tension when I'm anxious, and that can lead to pain."

"If the arm pain never worsened and other symptoms didn't show up, it can't have been anything serious."

"Except my body is stuck on the new anxiety symptoms now." Discouragement weighed her down.

Jayce squeezed her hand again. "What can I do?"

"I don't know, babe. Just keep being here for me, and be a voice of reason. It helps."

Part of Aria's left arm had hurt recently, and at first, she hadn't been sure why. She had been so nervous about having a heart attack that she made other pain appear in her chest and her back. Then tension traveled from her neck to her jaw to an area under her left eye. Aria finally remembered that she had been doing target practice with her bow earlier that day, which she hadn't done in a while. A muscle probably got strained.

But although the arm pain disappeared within an hour or so, the tension remained. By the next day, it became a new anxiety symptom. Pain in her left arm also sometimes joined the tension. Why couldn't the symptoms leave her alone?

Aria didn't tell her dad and Jayce about every physical symptom that worried her, but she was more open with them now. They were the rational minds that she needed when she couldn't trust her own. And they never got frustrated with her or made her feel ashamed, which was nice.

She hadn't even seen the healers for the pain or the tension. It took a lot of effort to go less. Telling her hyperawareness to stay calm was easier said than done. Aria let go of Jayce's arm as they walked across the courtyard.

"So what do you have going on next?" Jayce asked.

"Helping my dad with paperwork. Then we need to make preparations for the village visits tomorrow. But before we do that, I'm going to check on the progress of the new shaffron. We're trying out a prototype on Storm." Cold dread ran through her. "I don't like the thought of going to war."

"Me either. I don't think your dad and most of the other rulers are keen on it either, except Rodrick. But if push comes to shove, they won't have a choice. Bronson and Isabel were already swayed once."

They went into the castle, where it was cooler. A flight of stairs to the left led up to the next level. They had to go up two more floors to reach her dad's office.

"We were lucky that the seer wolves and the phoenixes helped to prevent the invaders from attacking us," Aria said. "I heard there were one hundred ninety phoenixes. Did anyone get a count on how many wolves came?"

"I heard there were eighty-five."

"I thought there had been one hundred, but I was so shocked by how large of a group showed up that I assumed there were that many. A lot more came than I expected. How many do you think there truly are?"

"I don't know, and I doubt we'll ever know. They guard their secrets well."

Aria quickened her pace. "Come on. My dad will wonder what's taking so long."

"When I marry you, will I have to deal with all of this paperwork?" Jayce had worry in his green eyes.

Aria smirked. "Do you really want to know the answer to that question?"

Jayce sighed, and his shoulders slumped. "I guess not."

Princess Aria has come a long way since surviving a near-death encounter with a wierlling and averting invaders in Torrannon, but the fight against mental illness can sometimes be one step forward, two steps back. As she struggles to overcome the health anxiety, her beloved horse, Storm, becomes lost in the wilderness.

Aria will once again have to find the strength to face more challenges and figure out new ways to get more control over her mind. She must also deal with the mysteries of why a strange man who she met on the road has a troublesome connection to her mother, Amelia, and why two panthers are too close for comfort.

The third book in the *Sparks Shall Rise* epic fantasy series is a tale about finding hope to keep fighting, even if the path ahead is stormy. Contains content dealing with suicide (off-screen), anxiety, and health anxiety.

Read Now

ABOUT THE AUTHOR

Lindsay McCafferty has been writing since she knew enough words to construct stories. After developing mental illness, she combined her passion with her torment. She hopes the tales and characters in the *Sparks Shall Rise* fantasy series will inspire others to find the courage and determination to rise above their own struggles, even if it seems impossible.

authorlindsaymccafferty.com

facebook.com/authorlindsaymccafferty

instagram.com/authorlindsaymccafferty

x.com/lindsaymauthor